TARNISHED

A NOVEL BY

Philip W. Hurst
and
J. Willis Hurst

LONGSTREET PRESS
Athens, Georgia

The story line of this novel is pure fiction. Some of the scenes described in the novel are based on events that actually happened, but in order to fit them into the story line, even they have been changed considerably. The scientific bases of the medical scenes are in line with the current understanding of the conditions that are discussed.

LONGSTREET
PRESS

Published by
LONGSTREET PRESS, INC.
325 Milledge Avenue
Athens, Georgia 30601
www.longstreetpress.net

Copyright © 2003 by Philip W. Hurst and J. Willis Hurst

1st printing, 2004

ISBN: 1-56352-716-2

All rights reserved. No part of this book may be reproduced in any form or by any means without the prior written permission of the Publisher, excepting brief quotes used in connection with reviews, written specifically for inclusion in a magazine or newspaper.

Printed in the United States of America

Jacket and book design by Burtch Hunter Design LLC
Jacket illustration by Burtch Bennett Hunter

To
Tamara and Nelie
Jessica, Christina, Jeffrey
And
John, Steve, and their families
With love

PREFACE

UNSEEN BY most individuals is the current health care *system* that consists of the good and bad interplay between: physicians; the law; business, including Health Maintenance Organizations; industry, including pharmaceutical houses; and politicians, including high officials in the federal government. Unfortunately the *system* is commonly flawed with unethical activity that in the long run prevents the delivery of services to individual patients or makes the cost of the service out of reach for many Americans. Good doctors are forced to work with their hands tied in a *system*, which is often filled with greed and unacceptable behavior. Admittedly, occasionally doctors fail to deliver services that the profession of medicine is noted for, but many times they are blamed for the unethical actions of another part of the *system*. When this occurs the doctor and the entire profession of medicine are tarnished.

As doctors and the profession of medicine are being tarnished by greed and unethical behavior by many external and internal forces, the *spirit of good doctors, nurses and other health care workers is slowly dying.* It is the hope of the authors that our novels, Prescription for Greed (2000) and Tarnished (2004), will shine some light on the tangled web and complexity of our growing health care issues. Hopefully, as a people we will *start over* and dedicate our efforts to building an excellent health care *system* that assures the public that each element of the system acts honorably without greed. *No unreasonable profits should be made from sick people.* The doctor must be a humanitarian as well as a scientist. The lawyer must not encourage patients to sue doctors and hospitals for frivolous reasons. The pharmaceutical houses must not gauge the pockets of patients. The politicians must not sell their integrity to help greedy elements of the system. Finally, a new approach to the financial support that is needed to care for the sick must be found. These attributes of a great health care *system* must be developed now because experts believe that health care will, within the next few years, account for 15-30 percent of America's economic output. Should this happen, as the authors believe it surely will—it may be impossible to start over.

We wish to give our special thanks to Errol Marshall who coached us on the current slang that is used in America and Craig Langford and Tamara Hurst, both wonderfully talented, who spent many hours reviewing and editing our manuscript. Tim Darnell, our chief editor, and Scott Bard, our publisher, made our work a reality.

We thank our wives, Tamara and Nelie, for tolerating our discussions over the last two years as we struggled to create this novel. Without their help and support this book could not have been written.

PHILIP W. HURST PH.D.
J. WILLIS HURST M.D.

TARNISHED

CHAPTER 1

NEW YORK CITY, NEW YORK
DECEMBER 2000

THE BOARDROOM of Speck MediSurge, a medical pharmaceutical and instrument company, had both the ambience and the smell of old money. The walls were dark oak polished to a fine shine. Brown leather chairs, made of the finest Argentine leather, were lightly worn from years of use and whispered luxury. The prize boardroom table was a masterpiece carved from rare African trees found only in "environmentally protected" areas of the rain forest. That table alone could fetch a hundred grand.

Yes, when you set foot in that boardroom the financial magnetism of Speck MediSurge immediately grabbed your psyche and filled it with dreams of wealth and power. More than one soul had been lost in this room.

Inhaling deeply, the CEO, Ronald 'Big Ron' Triplett, admired the view of New York City harbor. Watching a steady stream of ships crisscrossing the water gave him a moment of reflection. A moment he dedicated to calculating more ways to increase his financial empire.

There was something special about seeing the city from such an extremely elevated perspective. Looking down from a sixty-five floor high-rise made people look as insignificant as ants. And from the boardroom you could gaze down upon the hustle and bustle of the financial center of the city. There was always plenty of action in this city, day or night. And, of course, with the location of this building you could see the Statue of Liberty, majestic and symbolic in the distance. The view was particularly stunning when it was snowing softly as it was today.

Since the meeting was about to start, Triplett, as CEO of the company, stood next to the massive chair. His chair, his company. He found pleasure calling his subordinates together at the end of a long day for a meeting. He preferred long tedious meetings that lasted into the night. It sent a clear message to everyone that nothing was more important than business. Anyone who was concerned about workload, time with their family, or putting in too many hours, had better put a call into their headhunter.

There were twelve executive members in all. Each was there to present a quarterly report. Each had to justify in detail their budget, revenue, research investments, market trends, competition and strategy for the next quarter. Triplett expected, in fact he demanded to hear well thought out, solid, business plans.

Triplett made people nervous. Very nervous. Perhaps it was his piercing steel blue eyes that he used to break a person into submission. Or perhaps it was how he shifted his broad, tall body toward whoever was speaking. His hands were large and well manicured. His angular face had an intimidating hardness. Ever since college he had been mostly bald. What hair he had was white and groomed tightly against his head. He hated jewelry and was devoid of any, except for one large gold ring that bore an insignia of the globe. Sitting back in his chair he rubbed his ring and stared a hole into the person presenting. Financial goals and corporate results were his driving force. He didn't care how his people got there, only that they got there.

Triplett had grown up on the tough side of the city. His dad was a coldhearted man that rarely showed his son any affection. A handshake for a job well done was about as good as it got. Instead, he showed Ron how to survive the hard knocks of life. How to fight to get what he wanted. Fist, fury and smarts. That's what he grew up with every day. But most important was his dad's 'golden rule' that wealth belonged to the toughest player. Failure belonged to the weak.

Triplett's dad owned a big house where men with sunglasses and walkie-talkies were always walking the surrounding lawns and wooded areas. By the time Ron was fifteen he figured out that his dad, and his dad's partner, James Evian, who controlled the southern region, was connected to a well-established, very secret, crime syndicate. Key politicians, businessmen, and professional keepers of the peace were frequent visitors. A few years later his dad, whose health was failing, asked James Evian to take his son under his wing and become Ron's mentor. When the time was right, Evian was the man who would present Ron with the special gold leadership ring. A ring that only a few had earned.

Triplett's reflection abruptly ended when the others started to file into the room. As soon as Triplett sat down the boardroom became silent. It was a chilly silence. Slowly, he scanned the members of his board. They all carried a stern impenetrable look in their eyes. They all understood and cherished the corporate life and dedicated themselves to climbing the ladder of executive power. Most of them were void of any personal life and were as one dimensional in their aspirations as Triplett. The few who did attempt to live beyond work were the stepping stones of the others.

There was a lone woman at the table. Her name was Ruth; her enemies nicknamed her Ruthless. As an intellectual powerhouse she enjoyed making the cronies at the table sound confused and unprepared. She was the company's General Counsel and well suited for the job. Harvard JD/MBA, summa cum laude, unflinching in her drive. Her intellect was only matched by her cleverness for manipulation. Her firebrand chides of anyone attempting to cross her was well known and was the very reason why Triplett so enjoyed her presence. It certainly wasn't because she was a good-looking woman. She was five eight, square shaped, with a face that never broke into a smile unless she was pointing out a flaw in logic. Besides, it was well known that she preferred the company of her young female friends. Most men bored her with their bragging and strutting. The young females were easily shaped into fitting companions. She loved her job and devoured whatever fruits of life she desired.

One by one the members gave their updates. Each had hit their financial goals and each was given the all-important approving eye of Triplett. Indeed, this may be the best quarter of business in five years. The industry as a whole was doing well as pharmaceuticals and medical instruments were in high demand. New drugs and instruments were hitting the market at a blistering pace. New and improved versions of old cash cow products were coming out right and left. This was enough to make any CEO toast success. However, there was just one more item to attend to on the agenda before Triplett could stand and sing his own praises, announce bigger bonuses and, of course, celebrate. Just one more item.

The last agenda item was presented by Ruth. She was truly ruthless in her zealousness for boosting a competitive advantage of Speck MediSurge. Perhaps it was her upbringing that gave her so much drive. Brought up by foster parents who saw Ruth as a reflection of their so-called good will forced her to find creative ways to be recognized by others in the community. Often she would stir up a problem for someone and then be the one who saved the day.

At the age of seven Ruth teased a young boy next door into chasing her through the yard. As they passed by the corner of the house, Ruth saw that her foster dad had a pane glass door propped up waiting for installation. She took the turn a little wide and dodged the pane. The boy seeing a chance to cut her off ran into the glass. Blood spurted from his arms and face. It was Ruth who pulled the boy away and stopped the bleeding. She was proclaimed a marvel. Even the local newspaper praised her steadfastness and quick actions that saved the boy's life.

Now she was fire fighting the issues that threatened Speck MediSurge. Many didn't care for the fanatical tactics she employed under the guise of company protection, but despite this she was successful.

The last agenda item was about a security issue. Ruth called it, "flagrant disobedience of employees that could create a black eye on their branding efforts for years to come."

Speck MediSurge was neatly broken into two groups, "insider" employees who worked at corporate headquarters and "associates," the private practice doctors at medical centers who were paid by the organization to enter patients into various clinical trials. Everyone wondered which group she would target. Ruth was concerned with both. She claimed that insiders and associates were banding together and stirring up dissension in the ranks.

Primarily, several of their "associates" wanted to publish research findings independent of the Speck MediSurge review process. No one, but no one, was allowed to publish without internal review. Publishing unfavorable results could not be tolerated. Their competitors would blast them out of the industry. If a drug failed to produce expected results or created terrible side-effects internal protocol was to hide it and hide it well.

As soon as Ruth started to clamp down on those who were challenging the review process, one young researcher, an insider, secretly emptied his computer files and casually departed for lunch. Two days latter they were searching for him.

"What do you mean, took his disks and departed?" Triplett inquired.

"He took off with some computer disks." Ruth replied.

Triplett's blue eyes grew cold. "You mean to tell me that you let a researcher scoop up sensitive data and just walk out?"

"No," Ruth said, bracing for the attack. "It's not like that. He has been working with us for several years and he knew the security procedures extremely well."

"And why haven't you revamped our entire security system yet?" Triplett's voice was hardening. "You are the one who overlooks the legal and security division of our company. You are in charge of the system."

Ruth was not accustomed to being the one in Triplett's crosshairs.

Triplett's rather large fists were tightly balled. Nothing made him angrier than betrayal. "Who is it?"

"His name is Christopher Miller," Ruth replied.

"And just which pharmaceutical product was the young scientist working on?" Triplett's anger was very apparent.

"Actually, he was on two projects," Ruth took a deep breath and forced her gaze to remain steady. "The X-14 and the X…"

"And the X what?"

"The X-32, sir." Ruth looked down unable to meet Triplett's cold eyes.

The drugs were labeled for the mass market as Jorestat and Jorestat -2. Their names represented the union of Joint, Relief and Stat, which means immediate in the medical world. The 2 after the name was added a decade later because it was the second generation of the older drug.

The two drugs have almost identical chemical structures but their trade names showed the ingenuity of the advertising agency that named and marketed the drugs. Triplett hired a firebrand agency to get the names of Speck MediSurge drugs known throughout the world by advertising them in newspapers, magazines, television and radio. The agency was a real champ at capturing the people with arthritis using marketing statements that were just shy of being false.

Triplett didn't mind paying the agency mega bucks because he liked their method of operation. Besides, Triplett simply passed the cost on to the consumer. He even enjoyed giving mind-boggling bonuses to the agency when they skillfully marketed unapproved drugs without being caught.

Jorestat was an arthritis medication that had been around for twenty five years and was one of the best sellers for the company. However, there was a slight problem; Miller had information from numerous doctors in practice that Jorestat carried long term toxic side effects. The drug gradually destroyed the liver but Speck MediSurge had not discontinued advertising the value and safety of the drug. Jorestat -2, a newer version of Jorestat, was twice as powerful for dealing with arthritis and according to the MediSurge advertisements, it had fewer side effects. Miller had secret information about the new Jorestat -2 that actually showed that liver damage was occurring more frequently and quicker than it did with Jorestat. He had informed Ruth that the company should discontinue selling the drug, but Ruth didn't want to hear it.

Triplett was no longer a happy man. The good news from the last three hours of their meeting had just been overshadowed by one stupid security lapse. This quarter they may have reaped the most profit ever, but if that renegade scientist exposed the information on either of those two drugs, it could literally ruin the reputation of Speck MediSurge. Public perception and shareholder confidence would crash and an endless number of lawsuits would follow. Triplett could see the trial lawyer's fangs as they prepared their class action suits.

Triplett didn't tolerate sloppiness. Especially sloppiness like this.

Bonuses, hell, there would be a little house cleaning over this one.

The city snow crunched with each step that Christopher Miller took. He could barely see through the frosted lenses of his thick glasses. His frail physical frame made it difficult for him to march forward in the cold, but he knew that he had to keep moving. He could sense his predators, the security force of Speck MediSurge, getting closer. He realized now how stupid it was to have stopped by his apartment before leaving town, but he needed to get his passport and grab a few clothes before heading out to Mexico.

Yes, the Speck MediSurge boys were getting closer. Closer every minute. All that he could do was to keep moving. He clutched his computer briefcase tightly and chose to cut through a narrow alley. He knew that they were closing in quickly. He needed more time. Maybe he should hide. He looked and saw nothing but the brick walls of ancient rundown warehouses. He noticed a few old broken windows. Maybe he should climb through one and hide out till morning. They probably couldn't find him in a place like that. He tossed his small padded CD case through a lower window and jumped for the window ledge. The ledge was higher than he had anticipated. He would have to jump as high as he could just to grab the ledge.

"Hey." A loud shout crossed the alley. "There he is! Climbing into that window."

Their footsteps pounded closer as he struggled to pull himself up.

His adrenaline kicked up another notch. A few more inches and he would make it into the barren room. If only he were in halfway decent physical shape. If only he had made a better plan of escape. He was midway through the window when he felt a pair of vice-like hands clamp onto his ankles. He was losing his grip. In the dim light he could see his small CD case sitting on the floor of the warehouse.

Something moved.

There was something in the corner of the room next to the case. It moved again. Christopher struggled against the dark to see. It was a man. A homeless man curled up for warmth. Christopher saw the man pick up the CD case as the pull on his legs increased. He knew he was done for. He also knew what they would do to him. He whispered desperately to the homeless man, "Take it. Get outta here."

The homeless man edged his way closer. His eyes wide with fear. "Take it… Take it where?"

Christopher strained harder to hold on, his hands burned with the effort. "Get it to Bill Barringer in Atlanta."

"Barringer?"

"Yes, Dr. Bill Barringer," Christopher was now hanging on for dear life. Every muscle screamed with pain. He gave one last ditch effort to hold onto the ledge. One last thought, one last hope. "He'll pay you a lot of money for that case."

Those were Millers last words. Ripping him into the alley they rammed Miller's face into a stack of bricks cracking his front teeth, flattening his nose and driving his nose bone into his brain. Seconds later blood flowed over the alley bricks. Miller's pockets were searched, but nothing was found but keys and a wallet. No CD's.

When they reported back, Ruthless was left seething.

CHAPTER 2

ATLANTA, GEORGIA
DECEMBER 2000

TODAY OF all days.

It was one of the rare, truly harsh storms of the year in Atlanta. Heavy precipitation and a blasting cold front. At least by Atlanta standards the conditions were unbearable. As the storm crossed over the city, everything shut down tightly. The roads and bridges were covered with dangerously slick sheets of ice. It was cold and wet with a wind chill factor of ten below zero. Up north it would be just another storm, but in Atlanta it was downright cruel and unusual punishment. Driving was out of the question. Even walking was crazy. The city had essentially ground to a halt.

Today of all days.

Maybe it would warm up. After all it was still too early to tell if the sun was going to stand up to this mess and turn things around for Dr. William Barringer. He preferred to be called Bill by his friends and close colleagues. And Bill had been waiting for this day a long time. Too long for a storm to blow into the picture and ruin it. Everything was already planned, a simple informal ceremony with his soon to be wife, Connie, and the minister. No family. No friends. No headaches.

Bill stroked his sandpaper jaw and made his way toward the shower. He turned on the hot water and backed away, knowing that it would take at least five minutes to warm-up. He checked himself out in the bathroom mirror. He was wearing a pair of blue boxers, his bulky arms crossed with impatience.

His years as a doctor had been full of adventure. Starting out of the gate as a Vietnam field doctor. He had seen the pain and destruction that a body could endure. He was not the standard field doctor. His job sent him on special ops assignments behind enemy lines. He had to do more than know how to heal troops; he had to carry out deadly orders. Several times his group of specialists barely made it back. He carried a scar on his left side from one of those jungle assignments.

As he gazed in the mirror, he straightened up his six foot two inch frame. He looked and thought of himself as younger than fifty but it was apparent that a few changes were beginning to happen. It was harder to stay in shape. The beer and the barbecue did seem to stick to his ribs a little bit easier these days. Luckily he had always taken care of himself. His biggest physical complaint was a severe case of arthritis. His left shoulder had developed arthritis from too many high school football tackles. And his stiff knees were the result of the heavy take downs from his college wrestling days. Meds helped keep the pain in check. His reading glasses added to the perception of a comfortable middle aged man.

Bill leaned forward to stretch his back. His rugged face almost touched the mirror. Though the mirror was slightly fogged with steam he could easily see his receding hairline and the few wrinkles that traced the corners of his lips and eyes. Regardless, his dark brown eyes still looked both mysterious and mischievous. He smiled inwardly at the surge of youthful energy still projecting forth from within; a life force, aptly seasoned, and filled with purpose. He laughed out loud, somewhat surprising himself, "At least I've still got the old fire in the eyes..."

Steam had already curled up and covered the glass wall of the shower when the bathroom door cracked open. Connie poked her head in slowly. Although they had been living together for only a few months, their lives had intertwined off and on ever since they first met at Greystone University Hospital. In those days Connie was in medical school and Bill was completing his last year of medical residency. They were a little more than five years apart; the perfect time lapsed so that Bill could help her negotiate the myriad of political ropes within the medical school. Those early days, however, seemed like ages ago.

Since then, each of them had managed to fill their lives with complicated relationships from marriages that were never meant to be. But somehow that just made them appreciate each other even more, especially since their son John had come into their lives two years ago. Their lives had certainly twisted together in the strangest of ways. And now they were trying to keep it all together and do it right. In just a few hours Connie would officially drop her ex's last name and move on with her life as a Barringer.

Connie's road to success had certainly been bumpy. She seemed to trip over her own personal problems at every turn. Once she checked herself into a rehab center for alcohol. She had always had a fear of alcoholism. Growing up she saw her mother drink herself to death. She remembered how she stashed bottles of vodka around the house trying to hide how much she drank. But Connie knew. She would find a bottle of vodka under the bathroom sink where her mother would take her breakfast glass of grapefruit juice and add a morning eye-opener. She hated the way her mother's breath and sweat smelled like alcohol. It was sad to watch her self-destruct.

With her previous marital relationship constantly in a drama of accusations and fights and the pressure of starting a medical career, Connie noticed that she was having a few more cocktails in the evening. She could feel her control starting to ebb and she didn't want to run the risk of following her mother's footsteps. One day she woke up determined and checked into a facility to reestablish her identity.

Connie squinted as she encountered the brutally bright lights of the bathroom. She made her early morning faces and pawed at her short, black, silky hair. "So, tell me honey," she yawned and eased her way behind him. "Why is it that you've got to have the ceiling fan on in the middle of winter to go to sleep?"

Bill smiled, knowing that she hated to be cold. She always piled on extra blankets, but still never seemed to be warm enough.

"Hey, I'm no fool. You snuggle more when you're cold." Bill was taking in Connie's reflection in the mirror. He loved how her tall body, all five feet eleven inches, moved almost like a cat. She had a strong muscular back. Her waist, arms and legs were slender, but also strong. She too had been an athlete during her youthful school days. Her years as a college swimmer were still paying dividends. But it was her skin that he loved the most. Soft. Olive. Always smooth. Yes, it was her skin and her anciently enticing Italian eyes that really floored him. "Besides I can't breathe without the air stirring."

"Yeah, but you don't need a snow blower to breathe. And besides, the cold is always playing a number on your arthritis."

Bill walked over to her and gave her a quick hug of appreciation and changed the subject. "Honey, I'm afraid our big day may be spoiled. This storm is a killer."

Connie slipped by Bill and stole his shower. He laughed as he watched the warm water spraying on her shoulders and the nape of her neck.

"I'm glad we decided to have John boy stay here." They had debated whether John should go to the wedding or stay with old Jake who was the only employee of their little ranch. Connie rinsed her face and then continued, "I don't care if it does storm, as long as we have our wedding."

"Now you know why I bought that old Hummer for the ranch." Bill said proudly.

"You know living with you is like living with two people."

"What?"

"A sort of split personality."

"How's that?"

"Well, you're a doctor who works in the city of Atlanta driving a top of the line Lexus to work. You wear tailor-made suits and you love good restaurants. A true professional man."

"Don't forget the good looks." Bill slipped in quickly.

"Right, that too. But, then, you hate the city so you live out here on a ranch with horses. You are part mechanic and part home repair man, who wears nothing but blue jeans and boots and drives a Hummer."

Bill had owned the ranch for about twenty years. His land was located in the outskirts of Lawrenceville beyond Stone Mountain. Up to a few years ago there wasn't a lot of traffic. Today people were selling out right and left and it wouldn't be too long before the whole shebang would be just absorbed into Atlanta. But, he still had about a hundred acres. A hundred muddy acres at the moment.

"Mud and slick hills make a machine like my Hummer happy." As Bill reached over to the medicine cabinet to get his meds, he lowered his voice to reflect his determination. "Oh, our wedding is gonna happen alright. I'm gonna make sure of that."

Connie remained silent as she watched the steam develop into a thick, gray, swirling curtain. She poured some liquid lavender soap into her hand and smelled the deep rich aroma as it filled the shower.

Ok then, today of all days, nothing would be a problem.

The weather changed for the worse. But, true to his word, Bill's Hummer cruised over the messy terrain with ease as they headed for the church. He halfway deflated the tires going up the muddy slope of his unpaved driveway, but that was more for show than necessity. A simple push of a button inflated or deflated the tires. When they arrived at the church Bill was pleased to see that the minister, Reverend Josh Richardson, had made it and was just unlocking the front door of the small sanctuary. Seeing them drive up the Reverend stopped and waited for the couple to join him.

Reverend Richardson was a short, pleasant man in his mid-forties.

Although the Reverend was overweight by a good forty pounds, it seemed to suit him well. His head was round and full. He had bushy eyebrows that demanded your attention. Oddly, his feet and hands were small.

Of course, the Reverend had his frustrations. It wasn't easy trying to lead people to Christ. His own sister, Pamela, was perhaps his biggest heartache. She had not seen the light, so to speak, and she didn't seem to care. Pamela had always walked on the wild side of life. The last he heard she was still single, living in Washington, D.C. and hanging out with the inhabitants of the political jungle. For the last three or four years the tabloids were having a heyday portraying her as the beautiful escort of a top aide for Senator Adams. The pictures always presented her as a party animal. Reverend Richardson prayed for his younger red-headed sister every night. But, so far, his prayers remained unanswered.

The Reverend led the way to the front altar and stood before Connie and Bill.

Bill was expecting to feel nervous. At least sweaty palms and a thumping heart. After all, he had given up the idea of ever marrying again. He had two previous "mistakes" under his belt and he had been determined to stay a born-again bachelor. He smiled inwardly when a woman told him that he had an emotional wall around his heart. He remembered how they would get frustrated when they couldn't "reach" him. His dating scenes were like a repeating movie. Same lines. Same exits. Except for Connie. When Connie came back into his life, it was like an old memory that he'd just remembered for the first time. Two souls, not ready for each other as young adults but were destined to reconnect later in their lives.

Strangely, Bill felt very relaxed and then he felt himself swelling up pleasantly with joy.

Connie, too, looked at peace.

The service happened in a flash. Bill felt himself mouthing the words. They echoed in his mind. When the very last word was spoken, a wave of relief passed through him. A heavy burden lifted. Tears blurred his vision as he leaned forward and kissed his new wife.

Driving was easier now. The day had warmed up a little, maybe ten degrees or so and the cold wind was beginning to die down. They were more than a few blocks away from the church when Connie suddenly realized that they were heading in the wrong direction.

Calmly, Connie whispered. "Did the wedding make you disoriented or are you showing me a new way home?"

Bill kept his eyes on the road but tilted his head toward her. "I was wondering when you'd notice."

"So, are you planning to kidnap me and take me off to some tropical island?" Connie kidded.

"Nope."

"Are you thinking about a romantic spot in Paris?"

"No, don't think so."

"How about a ski trip to Beaver Creek, Colorado?"

"Beaver Creek?" Bill laughed.

"You know the place. Remember we were invited there last year to attend a medical conference?"

"You mean the freebie that Speck MediSurge was trying to get us to attend?" Bill replied with disdain. "Sorry, that's not my style."

"Hey, I wouldn't kick them too hard if I were you. After all they do produce those meds you take everyday." Connie defended. "Anyway, I remember the brochures about the resort. There is this wonderful spa and you can ski directly from the hotel to the lifts."

"And it probably costs about twelve grand a week." Bill pointed out. "All of which I'm sure a company like Speck MediSurge doesn't give a rats ass that it's passed on to the cost of medicine."

"I'm not talking about Speck MediSurge; I'm talking about us going there for a honeymoon."

Bill grinned knowing that he better go with her flow. "Sure, we can do that. Yeah, matter of fact we're heading to Beaver Creek right now." Bill looked at his watch. "We just have to catch the ten o'clock flight or we'll lose the trip."

Connie kissed his cheek. "That's a shame."

"Oh?"

"Yeah, because it's already noon, dear."

"Bummer, I messed up again."

Connie and Bill had actually already decided to postpone their honeymoon. Maybe in a few months.

"So, where are we heading?"

"We're heading over to celebrate with Vance and Jennifer."

Connie smiled.

Vance Connelly had been Bill's mentor. Not only of medicine, but also of life. To Bill, the now eighty year old "Chief" as he called him, was a perfect role model. Although Vance had long ago stopped admitting patients to the hospital, he continued to teach. Five days a week he could be seen at the crack of dawn making his way to his Greystone University Hospital office. Legend had it that if you touched the marble entrance sign of Greystone University Hospital at dawn some of the greatness of the university would rub off on you. Vance would occasionally stop and touch the sign. He would tell others that only those who had a love for medicine could feel the power emitted from the marble. At least, that was true for him.

The torch of leadership had been passed many years ago. Vance made sure that it was Bill who followed in his footsteps and became professor and chairman of the department of medicine. Since then it had been Bill's *modus operandi* to find Vance first thing in the morning, as often as possible, and have a cup of coffee with him. They called it their coffee conference; it never was a coffee break in the traditional sense. Small talk was rare.

When Bill and Connie arrived, Jennifer opened the door looking her characteristic spry self. She had been a nurse but she gave it up when she married Vance many decades ago. She admitted that medicine had passed her by. Now in her seventies her regal appearance was even more pronounced. Her shoulder length hair was a soft auburn-gray and she moved gracefully showing them the way to Vance's home-office, located in the kitchen. The kitchen table was piled with books, journals, papers, letters, an old laptop computer and the latest of Vance's own medical manuscripts. When they walked into the room Vance's wintered face lit up with pleasure.

Vance looked determined as always. A bit slower perhaps with his reflexes and just a bit smaller in stature these days, he was still obviously doing quite well with a strong and steady presence. His hair was his fountain of youth. It was still thick and a little wavy, vibrantly white and well groomed. His glasses were the same ones he had been wearing for the last twenty or so years, wire-rimmed bifocals. If anything, they only magnified his caring brown eyes. Although his walk had slowed a bit, he still had a good bounce to his legs and a firm handshake. He nodded to Jennifer, her cue to grab the champagne from the refrigerator. Walking directly to Connie, Vance embraced her fondly. "About time you two got your act together."

"Hey, I've always thought thrillers were the best acts," Connie stage whispered into Vance's ear as they finished their hug.

"Speaking of thrillers," Bill pointed to the journals and papers stacked on the table. "Whatcha working on now Vance?"

"I'm writing up an unusual case." Vance replied with an air of mystery.

While Jennifer slipped over to put a bottle of Dom Pérignon 1993 down on the counter and headed over to the cabinet to get crystal champagne glasses, Bill inquired. "So tell us about the case." He enjoyed a good medical brainteaser.

Vance's smile brightened knowing they would inquire. "Oh, it's about a rare cause of heart disease." Vance had made a career of studying nature on a rampage. Learning the secrets of the most unusual cases seemed to increase his knowledge of the more common ones.

Vance flagged them to look into the den. "See that afghan over there on the sofa?"

Connie was impressed with its beauty.

"The patient I am reporting on in this manuscript just sent it to me. This wonderful lady made it herself."

"Imagine the hours that took." Bill admired. "I'd say it's worth a pretty penny."

Vance disagreed. "No that's wrong. It's priceless because it reflects her gratitude for the diagnoses I made. "

Bill wasn't surprised with that answer. That answer was vintage Vance. "So give us the scoop, what prompted you to write up her case?" Bill pushed.

"Here, I'll show you this part, but I'll hold back on the conclusion." Vance handed Bill his personal notes about the patient. Connie leaned on Bill's shoulder to get a view.

Mrs. Sarah Wells
April 6, 1980
The patient was a 61 year old caucasian female.

Doctors from Jacksonville Florida initially diagnosed the patient as having liver disease due to the drug Jorestat that the patient had been taking for some type of arthritis for the last five years and had recently developed a large liver. The doctors were concerned because they had heard of another patient who developed liver disease while taking the drug. Because of that they studied the patients liver extensively. They concluded after their studies that her liver was simply swollen from congestion and that there was no evidence the drug had caused the problem. To be safe they recommended that the

> patient stop taking the drug. The doctors referred the patient to Greystone for further study.
>
> The patient reported occasional flushing of the face. In addition to a large liver the patient had severe heart failure. The patients right ventricle was dilated and the heart valve leading to the pulmonary artery was severely damaged. The patient had excess fluid in her abdomen.
>
> Flushing plus the disease of the right ventricle can occur when a carcinoid tumor of the small intestine metastasizes to the liver. When such a tumor has spread to the liver the venous drainage takes the toxic substance it produces to the right side of the heart where it produces disease of the heart valves and the inner lining of the right ventricle. However as long as the tumor is localized to the small intestine the toxic substances are destroyed by the liver. Her liver was enlarged due to congestion and there was no evidence that the carcinoid tumor had metastasized to the liver.

Bill and Connie finished reading Vance's notes and stepped back in puzzlement.

"This doesn't make sense," Bill reread the last part of the case notes. He looked to Vance for a clue. "If there was no abnormality of the liver except for congestion, then the tumor in the small intestine hadn't spread to the liver. So how did the toxin get to the heart?"

Vance remained stone-faced as he watched them struggle.

"The toxin had to have a direct path to the heart." Connie said thinking aloud.

Vance encouraged her thinking. "So what path could that be?"

She snapped her fingers and with some excitement said, "I know. The original tumor was in the ovary. The venous drainage from the ovaries goes directly to the heart."

"Damn!" Bill balled his fist. "I should have remembered that. It must have been the wedding; I was obviously distracted."

"Oh no you don't." Connie headed him off. "I won fair and square."

Jennifer held up the bottle champagne. "So, now that the game is over can we get back to celebrating?"

Vance handed them the reminder of his notes.

> Cardiac surgeons inserted a new heart valve that improved the patients heart failure. GYN surgeons removed the left ovary where the tumor was located.
>
> The patient holds the record for long term survival and has only had a few problems since surgery.

Vance had to summarize the case first. He revealed his motivation for writing the article. "I'm writing up this case to remind those who teach medicine the value of knowing good old fashion anatomy. In this case it was necessary to remember that the venous drainage of the ovary went directly to the heart." He pointed to a letter on the top of a stack of papers. "I just wrote her a note to thank her for the afghan and tell her what a pleasure it has been to know her."

"I can tell you one thing that caught my attention in this case." Bill pulled out a pill from his pocket. "I always carry one of these for my arthritis. But, to my knowledge Speck MediSurge hasn't reported any liver damage from taking Jorestat or Jorestat -2."

"We better keep our eyes open." Connie said concerned.

"Just the same I think I'll go off the stuff until we find out for sure." Bill replied.

Jennifer was standing next to the counter with a bottle of Champagne in her hand. "Ok, enough shoptalk. I think it's time to pull the cork."

After a push with Vance's thumbs and the soft pop of good

champagne they toasted to success and happiness. Even Connie decided to have a few sips. By the time they finished their first bottle, they had run out of toasts, but not champagne. The second bottle was opened and they savored every sip.

Jennifer had planned ahead making sure they had plenty to eat. She had an adequate spread of jumbo gulf shrimp, Cornish Game Hen salad, Virginia Wild Ham, rare roast beef and a deli shop medley of the finest cheeses. But Jennifer's homemade breads stole the show. Many glorious hours later with stomachs full, good cheer all around, and smiles on everyone's faces, the Barringer's set their course for home. Their hometown honeymoon had started off with a hit.

CHAPTER 3

JACKSON, MISSISSIPPI
JANUARY 2001

IN JACKSON, Mississippi, the sun gave up its battle for the sky and happily resigned without a struggle. Colors faded quickly, twilight was waving its dull gray flag. It was the balancing point in the battle between the colors of day and the darkness of night. A powerful natural display, mirroring the way Senator Chase Adams viewed the world. He was glad to see nightfall hitting his great state of Mississippi. He always preferred darkness. He enjoyed staying up through the early hours of the morning and then sleeping until noon. Cigars and fine wines tasted much better, people were more interesting, and politics was definitely more captivating during the night.

The next session of U.S. Congress wouldn't start until next week. Usually the first few days were crazy. Senator Adams always enjoyed the start of a new session; especially when he had control of a bunch of first term senatorial rookies. There was nothing sweeter than taking a few young senators under his wing and piling up a few owed favors from them early in their career. Favors had been his main ticket to power for over thirty years. Of course, manipulations always followed the favors. His methods were like the old style politicians and he was a true professional at the ancient art.

On Capitol Hill, Adams was known as the "Catfish". In his early years he was referred to as "Cat" Adams because he could detect the whims of the popular vote so quickly. His instincts were solid. His patience was admirable. And somehow he always landed on his feet. But as time passed, his true nature became apparent and someone added the "fish" part because whenever Adams was involved things began to smell, like the time he destroyed a long standing senatorial friend by revealing the man's gambling addiction. To Adams it was justified because a true friend would have supported Adam's pork barrel legislation.

He was an overweight, stringy haired, dangerous, egotistical man of wealth and power. Lots of power. Adams was pleased with himself and his station in life. He liked playing hardball.

Senator Adams loved his close of the day cocktail and he was getting impatient to sip his favorite single malt scotch. He liked to double the dose and then thumb through a few newspapers. He only read articles that grabbed his attention. Typically he would have already finished a couple of drinks by now, but his doctor had prescribed a tranquilizer for his stress and also told him to stop drinking. He stopped drinking for about two weeks and then found that he felt better to drink after all. Today however was different. He would need his wits today.

Shortly he would be meeting with his biggest campaign supporter, Big Ron Triplett. This wasn't a social visit. This was business. Serious business.

Senator Adams was one of the few people that knew Triplett's real identity. In reality Triplett was far more than just a CEO of a company. He was affiliated with the Association of Global Opportunity Seekers, simply called the Association for short. Triplett's dad helped to pioneer the Association and it had grown into an international crime syndicate. The senator knew that the Association was showing their greatest respect for him by sending Triplett. He was the highest-ranking officer in the Association that Adams had ever met one-on-

one. Triplett was in charge of operations for white-collar fleecing in the United States. Not crime, but fleecing. Crime was a totally different division. Triplett had to create swindling methods to get money for the Association.

Adams knew Triplett enjoyed intimidating people with his powerful build, steel blue eyes, and oppressive reputation, and so he had created the most oppressive atmosphere imaginable for his meeting with the crime syndicate boss on the deck of his indoor heated pool. He even had extra steam piped into the room, to make the occasion even more uncomfortable for his guest. The senator was looking forward to seeing the egotistical bastard sweat.

The senator was comfortable in his swimsuit and light bathrobe. The warm, moist air and tropical plants made the room feel like a jungle. The senator thought of it as a huge steam room. For this occasion he kept a chilled towel wrapped around his neck. Triplett would at least be physically uncomfortable if he tried to intimidate the senator. Perhaps on the senator's turf they would be equal. Perhaps here Triplett would be the one who sweated the most.

The pool was located on the western side of Adams' country estate. His mansion sat quietly on top of a rolling hillside revealing a beautiful view that stretched for miles. It was from that vantage point that he saw a limo round the first bend of his mile-long, winding driveway.

"Neil Henry!" The senator shouted when the limo rounded the next to the last bend. "Neil, get ready to greet our guest. And turn up the steam."

Neil Henry was forty-seven and had been the senator's chief of staff for the last decade. He was the serious type who skipped several grades during his academic career and was a whiz with statistics. A political strategist of the highest caliber. Just recently he had laser surgery on his eyes and he gratefully tossed away his glasses. His body wasn't frail, nor was it imposing to other men. Especially when he stood next to one of the senator's bodyguards. The guards were all ex-military, upright and uptight; they would kill on command. Neil Henry had never handled a weapon, and probably never would.

Neil watched the limo pull up to the covered entrance to the mansion. Two men got out of the car. A couple of tree trunk necks that sloped into massive shoulders. They seemed to be comfortable in their black cashmere coats, dark glasses and black leather gloves. They glanced furtively around. They were Triplett's bodyguards. They took their time approaching the front door. Now for the security checks. A ritual that both sides would perform.

Close to ten minutes later a bald man stepped out of the limo. Triplett himself.

Everyone who knew the story of Triplett understood why he had bodyguards. When he was young he cut his teeth as a bookie and loan shark as a way to work himself through college. He was a risk taker, but rumor has it that his mentor, James Evian from the Association watched proudly, never allowing anything serious to happen to the young man.

James Evian was indeed proud of Ron's prowess and made sure Ron's dad knew each step his son took. That's why Ron was taken under the wing of his mafia father's number one man. Ron's dad was just as daring in his youth. But his dad saw more than a risk taker in his son, he saw the future. The association needed to train their future officers in a new way of doing business. That's when his dad created the fleecing side of the business. A perfect spot for Ron.

His dad didn't have to give the hard sell to convince his son to join the Association. Ron was a natural at putting together mega-deals that were legal, but very shady. Now, after more than fifty years with the Association, he was at his zenith. He was a leader in the Association with the perfect cover, a CEO of a respected firm. He gave orders that went through the many chains of his network. He was essentially insulated beyond the reach of the law.

Neil Henry opened the door and welcomed Triplett.

Triplett strolled into the room filling it with his presence. A commanding tower of strength over Neil.

As soon as they reached the pool area, Neil thought he saw a smile on Triplett's face. A smile of curiosity. Triplett's bodyguards were present, yet trying to be invisible. The steam, however, was already penetrating. They began to sweat almost immediately. They took off their overcoats and gloves and handed them to Neil, who simply tossed them onto the nearest chair.

"Hello Senator." Triplett said casually.

"Well now, Mr. Triplett," the senator remained seated. He knew that Triplett would normally stand close by and look down at him. Instead of getting up and shaking hands the senator pointed to a chair and motioned for Triplett to have a seat. Of course, there was only one reasonably tall chair. And that chair was occupied by the senator. "I believe you're just in time for some refreshments."

At first the senator wasn't sure if Triplett was going to have a seat. But eventually Triplett put his six foot three inch, 240-pounds gingerly into the chair. They were now at eye level with each other.

"Yes, of course." Triplett replied. "I'd love a drink."

The senator looked at Neil. "I'd like my usual."

"Single malt scotch neat?" Neil confirmed.

"Of course."

Triplett noticed that the senator ordered first. Rudeness was a quality that irritated him. The senator had done his homework. But, then again, Triplett had done his.

"And you Mr. Triplett?" Neil asked.

"I'd like three fingers of Jack Daniel's with a splash of Diet Coke."

The senator frowned. "Whiskey and Diet Coke?"

"Each to his own, Senator."

The senator gave a short smug laugh. "Well, Triplett, I'm the type that likes to cut through the bull and lay the cards on the table."

The senator glanced at Triplett's two bodyguards. They were sweating through their shirts. Triplett still had his overcoat on and appeared cool and collected. The senator wondered if Triplett was really miserable under that coat. He didn't appear to be, but was he?

Triplett decided to play his own irritating game with the Senator. Out of the blue Triplett told the senator that a good friend of his was recently buried. Triplett's "good friend" headed the biggest white-collar crime association in New York. "Good friend" was a euphemism; Triplett didn't have any good friends or really many friends at all.

"My friend was at a restaurant." Triplett deadpanned. "Apparently when he went to the men's room somebody decided to help him with his tie."

"You mean he was strangled?" The senator asked.

Triplett's face remained clear of any emotion as he explained, "No, somebody gave him a Colombian neck tie." Triplett leaned forward and looked into the senator's eyes. "Someone slit his throat and pulled his tongue through the slit."

Fear instantly entered the room and squeezed the senator's heart.

He could feel a thick lump in his throat, making it difficult for him to swallow, much less speak.

Triplett stood and looked down at the senator. "Hey, it was his favorite Italian place. I'm sure he died a happy, full man."

Swiping his towel across his brow, the senator noticed that the towel had lost its chill.

Neil returned with the drinks and the senator gulped his in two swallows.

"Now, now Senator," Triplett looked surprised. "Polishing off a fine scotch whiskey like it was bar room tequila?"

"Neil, I'll take another one." The senator stated without responding to Triplett's comment.

"Senator, I have come today to tell you some bad news."

The senator eyes narrowed as they focussed on Triplett.

Triplett tried to look sympathetic. "The Association has decided it's time for you to retire."

"Me, retire?"

"Yes, it's time."

The senator looked at Neil. "Imagine that. The Association has decided that I should get out of politics."

"That's ridiculous, Senator." Neil handed his boss another scotch. Neil continued to talk as he refreshed Triplett's drink. "The senator has been in office for decades and has delivered his vote, and the vote of many of his colleagues, in favor of every major legislation that the Association wanted."

"Senator you've been getting too much bad press." Triplett said calmly. "It started a few years ago and it's been going downhill ever since. You were the chairman of the health committee. " He took a sip of his drink. "You were a joke. I've never seen such a mishandled job in my life. You barely escaped a Grand Jury investigation because of that screw up. And when you went in front of the Senate Ethics Committee you made headlines for a year. The wrong headlines for our purpose! Hell, it was because you couldn't stop that old doctor, Vance Connelly, from creating such a stir about health care that got Hillgren elected President."

"Hillgren, our so-called wonderful president, is our worst nightmare. We may even have to-" Triplett stopped short of telling what the Association was considering.

"Health care was just one point that helped Hillgren." Neil said defensively.

Triplett looked at Neil sternly. "It was the major part of his platform, you idiot."

Neil didn't want to banter on this issue anymore. Instead he sat down into a nearby chair.

Triplett stood to take off his overcoat. "As a matter of fact, the Association should have pulled the plug when the senator here had to go in front of the Senate Ethics Committee. God only knows how you bribed or threatened your way out of that one. Now practically everybody in the whole damn country knows how we fleece the medical system."

Triplett looked down at the senator. "Look at it this way Senator; we have decided that you earned your retirement."

The senator understood that message. Retire willingly or retire permanently. He needed time to stall, to somehow keep his cool and turn this situation around.

The Catfish felt his reign of power slipping away. He needed a way out.

For the first time the Catfish didn't have any mud for hiding and his face was clean of his usual predatory grin.

"Who goes into my slot?" The senator asked in a flat monotone voice.

Triplett rather perversely enjoyed sharing the plans. "The governor will make the appointment as to who will replace you."

"And, of course, that will give him several years as an incumbent instead of having to start fresh." Recognition is the biggest battle of politics. "And who will the governor appoint?" Senator Adams pressed.

"Charles Henderson." Triplett replied.

The senator bolted upright.

"He's perfect. He's well known and well received in this state." Triplett knew well that the senator and Henderson had been political enemies for decades. In fact they'd had a bitter campaign the last go around. And, it went without saying that Henderson now owed his soul to the Association.

The Catfish was stunned.

He was down, but not out.

———◄o►———

Pamela Richardson was handpicked by Neil Henry to help with the day-to-day operations of the senator. She was sexy, redheaded, and an administrative and computer whiz. The kind of gal that made most men and a lot of women squirm for her attention. Her motivation was purely Pamela. She had proven herself a valuable asset to the senator many times over.

Neil's plan was to have Pamela enter the pool area after about an hour or so of Triplett's visit. She was a decoy. Someone who could divert Triplett's focus from business and perhaps give the senator a slight edge.

Pamela was wearing a short silk robe over her bikini. The vivid colors of her robe were striking and played well with her emerald green eyes. The bodyguards appeared dazed. The sound of her high heels broke the silence.

"Well, well," Triplett admired. "Who do we have here?"

"She works side by side with me." Neil spoke up.

"I'll bet she does." Triplett replied, his voice low and soft.

Neil didn't care for the way Triplett stared at Pamela. He appraised her like she was a truck stop stripper. The polished businessman act eroded into the decadent bully that he was. Maybe her diversion would work better than the senator's excessively heated pool idea.

After introductions Neil told Pamela about Triplett's news. She didn't even blink. She simply arched her right eyebrow and glanced at Triplett. "Well, seems like you boys don't beat around the bush. I was expecting to be celebrating with you."

Triplett was still admiring Pamela. "No reason we can't celebrate. It's not every day the senator decides to have a career change."

"Somehow I don't see the senator doing anything but politics." Pamela retorted.

"Come now," Triplett tried to ease the moment. He edged closer to Pamela. Although she was tall, her head just came even with his chest. Triplett spoke softly to Adams while still gazing at Pamela. "Senator don't you belong to four or five country clubs?"

The senator gave a half nod.

"See there," Triplett said, "I'm sure the senator wants to improve his golf game."

A cell phone rang from the pocket of one of Triplett's bodyguards. After turning his head away from the group he answered the phone with a hoarse rough voice. He held the phone to Triplett and in a hushed voice told him that Henderson was on the line. Apparently Triplett would be going to meet Henderson next.

Triplett completed his call within a couple of minutes and then said, "Well, sounds like the next senator of Mississippi is anxious to meet with me."

"I guess since you're in the neighborhood," Senator Adams used his most polite southern drawl as he shook the ice cubes in his glass, "you ought to stop by and congratulate your newest recruit."

Pamela could read the senator. Whenever he sounded calm and collected, but constantly shook his glass, she knew she needed to buy some time for him. Slowly she took off her robe and removed her high heels. "I guess I might as well enjoy the pool." She brushed by Triplett and suggestively walked to the water, and tested the temperature with her toe.

They watched as she eased herself into the warm water. She bent her knees and allowed the water to reach her neck. Then she stood and casually brushed the droplets off her arms, allowing her audience to see the chilling aftereffects prominently displayed through her sheer suit top. She was wading waist high when Triplett got the urge to join her. He wasn't really the shy type. At his place, he'd even used the same heated pool trick that the senator was trying to pull here. At his pool he'd go skinny-dipping and challenge the others to do so as well. Embarrassment is a powerful weapon.

Not today, however. Today this sort of stunt would be more advantageous to the senator. Triplett would look like a fool. Instead he asked politely for a bathing suit and a place to change.

When he returned his physical presence was even more pronounced. Now even Pamela was a bit intimidated. He dove in and stood in water that was too deep for her. She swam up to him and used his broad shoulders as support. The others could barely see through the steam of the pool and their conversation was muddled. The waterfall provided excellent cover for all conversations.

Triplett large hands held Pamela just up above the water. He squeezed until he saw her wince. He pulled her slowly closer to him. "You know, a sharp woman like you could have a job in my company."

"Your company or the Association?"

Triplett laughed.

"Thanks, but I don't think now is the time." Pamela turned her body and he drew her to him. She could feel his strong chest as his arm wrapped around her waist.

"What's to keep you around here?"

"I'm not sure you really want the senator out of the picture yet."

"Oh, why is that?"

Pamela swayed from side to side lightly stroking against Triplett. "Well, you see, the senator may be drawing some heat these days, but I wouldn't count him out just because of that."

"I'm listening." Triplett didn't want her to stop rubbing against him. He moved his arm higher, his thumb stroking the underside of her breast.

"Well, the senator has a few special accounts that you might be interested in knowing about." Pamela paused long enough to highlight, "I know that at least one goes to Hillgren's top man."

"Vice President Lancaster?" Triplett smoothly inquired.

"He was the president's choice for VP and he is the president's closest top advisor." Pamela lied about the special account for the vice president, but she knew that would get Triplett's attention.

Triplett reluctantly stopped Pamela's little water dance and turned her to face him. "Why didn't he say anything about this to me?"

"I don't know for sure, but if I were you I wouldn't replace the senator with a dumb animal like Henderson."

"And how do you know all this?" Triplett figured they weren't telling Pamela everything.

Now Pamela was smiling. "I'm not all looks you know. I know a lot about computers, too. I put a Trojan horse into the senator's computer system."

"What's a Trojan horse?"

"In the computer world it's sort of like a virus that attaches to your information highway and retrieves information for you…sort of sucks the information right up, you might say."

"The senator can't detect it?"

"Nope."

"How often do you retrieve the information?"

"Anytime I need an update of a certain activity."

"Like bank activity?"

"Precisely."

Triplett released Pamela and started swimming slowly toward the senator. Pamela was keeping close by him. She could see that this was the sort of break that Triplett was looking for to control the Hillgren administration.

Triplett lifted himself out of the water with little effort and walked over to the Catfish. "Mind if I borrow one of those towels, Senator?"

Neil quickly handed him the towel that had been chilled in an ice cooler. Triplett didn't seem to care. He simply wrapped it around his body and started to walk back over to Pamela. He helped her out of the pool and whispered into her ear. "And why are you telling me all of this?"

She whispered back. "Like you said, I may someday need a new position and I just want you to know all of my talents." She paraded in front of everyone to get her robe and shoes.

Triplett looked back at the senator and Neil. "Mind if I stay the night Senator?"

The senator was smoking his usual Cuban cigar. "Thought you were going to Henderson's for the evening?"

"I've decided to think my plan over a bit, Senator."

"You mean that you may have had a change of heart?"

"Yes, I may have been a little hasty in my original suggestion."

"I see." The senator was puffing on his cigar with great pleasure. "I think it's worth your consideration for at least one evening."

The Catfish winked his eye and told Pamela to help Triplett find the main guestroom.

Now Pamela could demonstrate her other talents.

In the morning Triplett left the mansion. Some major decisions had been made. He had decided to return to his condo in Ponte Vera, Florida. He didn't visit Henderson. Instead he talked to him on the phone. Essentially he told Henderson that the senator was getting a second chance. Henderson's senatorial bid was put on hold for a while, possibly a long while.

During the night, between their episodes of passion, Triplett listened to Pamela and developed a plan. She would be his insider ready on his command to deliver all types of services. She agreed for a price, a very big price.

The Catfish was overjoyed at sticking it to Henderson. But his greatest pleasure was hearing Triplett give him a second chance. Triplett told the senator that his number one priority was keeping the health care system the way it was. Triplett made it clear that he didn't want another botched medical scandal. And with Hillgren trying to reform the medical system, the senator would have plenty of opportunity to regain his favor.

The Catfish was grinning again.

Triplett took it hook, line and sinker. Of course, the story about the Vice President being bought off with a special account was a bluff. Pamela had learned long ago not to reveal the real angle. But, there was some hidden truth that lurked within her story. Neil Henry did have an angle on the Vice President, but Pamela wasn't going to give away their hand that easily.

CHAPTER 4

ATLANTA, GEORGIA
FEBRUARY 2001

THE WEATHER was kind for February. No rain. No cold winds. A little on the gray side and chilly enough to wrap up in an overcoat. Vance was sitting at his office desk, taking a short break. He enjoyed looking out the window to see if the doctors walking into Greystone would touch the marble sign. He saw Bill give it a good tag. Today Vance and Bill were meeting with the interns who were beginning their rotation on the cardiology service the following week. When possible they liked to meet them individually. Vance was particularly interested in meeting with Quincy T. Watts.

Quincy was quiet and low-key. His personality was similar to Bill. His background, however, was very different. Like many African-American professionals, Quincy had learned to keep an emotional and suspicious distance from those in charge. He believed the higher he climbed the ladder, the more others seemed to think it was because he was given preferential treatment rather than because he possessed talent and ability. He was tired of those battles and he was tired of carrying a chip on his shoulder because of them.

Bill gave a tap on Vance's door before walking into the office. Vance kept his attention on the marble slab outside, so Bill quietly sat down in his usual chair.

Vance had always used a round table for his office desk. He felt like it made his office friendlier and it was designed to obtain more input from others. A traditional office desk had always seemed too authoritarian seemingly designed for power plays and separation. Vance didn't need or want the props.

"You got something on your mind, Vance?" Bill asked.

"No, I'm just watching."

Bill stood up and looked outside where he thought Vance was looking. He watched as a steady stream of people crossed the street in front of the hospital. Then he noticed Quincy standing with some nurses and other hospital employees. He stood out from the crowd looking tall and lean. He must be cracking jokes, you could see him laughing and smiling. "You're watching Quincy?"

"Sort of." Vance watched Quincy just like he diagnosed a patient. His right eye squinted and he had a far off look in his left eye. He was examining Quincy for more than his twenty-six year old vigor; Vance was watching how the intern interacted with his friends. Vance noticed that the others sort of huddled together, all facing Quincy. He also noted that when Quincy took a few steps and the huddle followed. True, Quincy was a good-looking man. He was strong, standing over six feet tall with facial features that set the stage for his awesome smile. Even at a distance, Vance could see that Quincy was a natural leader.

They watched as Quincy said goodbye to his friends. He was running five minutes late. He checked his watch and picked up his pace. He crossed the street and bee lined it toward the hospital.

Vance stood up and watched intensely. "This is the part I wanted to see." Reflexively Quincy gave the entrance sign a high five. It looked smooth and well practiced. A smile beamed across Vance's face. "I've been watching doctors for years as they make their way into the hospital and very few develop the habit of tagging the entrance sign."

Eight minutes late and counting.

Vance looked at Bill, "By the way, what made you develop that habit?"

Bill wasn't surprised that Vance knew that he tagged the sign. "Perhaps, I wanted a way to anchor myself."

"In what way?"

"The sort of anchor that would remind me," Bill felt like his response would sound a silly, "that a lot of doctors paved the way here and set high standards for us."

Vance smiled and nodded.

Bill checked his watch again. Usually Vance would show his type A behavior by now. Instead, Vance was calm as he walked to the door.

At nine minutes and thirty seconds into the count down, Quincy rapped on the door. He only hit it once before Vance snatched it open.

Quincy's second strike hit nothing but air.

"Good afternoon, Dr. Watts." Vance said as he walked back toward his round table.

"Well, sir—"

"Please, no excuses." Vance sat down and picked up the folder that had Quincy's life history. Vance looked perturbed. "I make it a practice to always be early at a meeting, Dr. Watts."

"Well I—"

Vance interrupted. "I think it's important to show respect for other people's time. Also, I have always worried that the habit of tardiness in interns and residents might carry over to believing that it is acceptable to keep patients waiting."

Bill flagged Quincy to take a seat as he explained. "Starting next week you'll be spending your early mornings with Dr. Connelly and me."

Quincy half smiled at Vance as if he were looking forward to it. He did love his sleep though.

Vance held up Quincy's resume. "I see you were born and raised in Auburn, Alabama. You stayed there and attended Auburn University."

Vance thumbed through the resume. It was a stall tactic to see if

Quincy needed to fill the void of silence with chatter.

Instead of speaking, Quincy sat quietly and thought about his dad and mom. Quincy was the first in his family to finish college. His mom and dad had finished high school but then started a family. They both were hard working parents and good Christians. They taught Sunday school and walked the straight and narrow. No drinking. No cursing. They tried to bring up their four children the same way.

Finally Vance looked up and continued talking. "I see that you had a major in archaeology."

"Yes, I also had a double minor in biology and chemistry."

Vance thought it was better when doctors had diverse backgrounds. He worried that the doctor world was becoming to homogenous.

"Looks like you did well there." Vance said.

Quincy nodded.

"What attracted you to archaeology?" Vance asked.

"Probably saw one too many action movies." Quincy gave a big smile as he recalled the action films of his youth.

Vance didn't appear to be entertained by Quincy's comment.

Clearing his throat, Quincy settled down to give a serious reply. "Because I like the idea of knowing things that most people don't have a clue or inclination to know about."

"An expert of some sort?"

"Yes, I knew I had to be a specialist of some kind."

Vance liked to talk about an intern's interests outside of medicine. It furthered his insight into the person's character. He knew from Quincy's record that he was very bright, asked himself questions and pursued the answers, stayed abreast of the issues, and occasionally exhibited signs of being a sharp diagnostician. These are some of the traits needed if someone wanted to break out from the pack and become a leading physician.

"Seen as an expert as opposed to?" Vance pressed.

"Getting a position because I'm African-American."

Bill asked. "You believe that's what people think now that you're a doctor?"

"Sometimes."

"Why?" Vance wasn't one to let something slip by. He wanted it on the table.

Quincy picked his words carefully. "When I got accepted to medical school, there were a lot of people acting as if I made it just because I was an Affirmative Action candidate. I felt like a lot of white college students got mad because they figured that I was taking up their slot. They assumed they were more qualified than me."

"And what about yourself?" Vance took a few notes. "Do you believe they were more qualified?"

"No, I don't."

"Why is that Quincy?" Vance was like a bulldog. He simply wouldn't let go.

Quincy leaned forward and stared directly into Vance's eyes. "I had the grades. I had the extra-curricular activities. There was no reason for anyone to doubt my qualifications."

Vance appreciated forthrightness as they continued to hold eyes.

Quincy eased back into his chair. He realized there was no room for stealth with Vance or Bill. He was awed that Vance had pulled so much out of him.

Vance had a bit of a grin on his face. There was a certain edge to Quincy that Vance liked. A little pent up anger, coupled with a strong sense of desire for learning. They spent the next thirty minutes talking about medical school and the subjects that most intrigued Quincy.

Clearly Quincy understood the scientific part of medicine, but he had to apply it to his patients. He also had to understand that medicine was a humanistic endeavor. Vance could tell that the heart side, the caring for others, was within Quincy, just a bit hidden. This was the type trainee that Vance enjoyed the most. He was the one in a hundred that Vance expected to go to the next level.

"You tell me Dr. Connelly. What does my record look like?"

Vance pushed aside the resume. He slowly got up and walked over to his coffeepot and poured a cup. Black coffee. No available cream or sugar. Everyone had to have it black. Vance delivered the coffee and resumed the conversation.

"This is what your resume tells me." Vance stood as he talked. "You've spent four years in medical school and you've done a good job learning the language of medicine. But don't confuse learning the language and knowing a great deal of facts with being a skilled doctor."

Quincy listened as he drank his coffee. The coffee was old, thick and strong. Quincy wasn't about to say that he had tasted better instant coffee in a truck stop. Instead, he smiled after each sip belying the grimace he felt inside.

Vance continued, "You're not skilled yet. That's not a derogatory statement because no medical school graduate is skilled. That's why we have internships and residency programs."

Quincy calmly took another sip of coffee. His taste buds recoiled.

"It's the next three to six years of training in the hospital that will give you the chance to perfect the skills you'll need." Finally Vance took a sip of coffee and almost spit it out. His face soured. "Good grief. This stuff is awful." He set it aside. "Why didn't you guys say something?"

Vance wiped his mouth with a paper napkin and watched Quincy finish his coffee.

"I figured this was just another test of some kind." Quincy put his empty cup down. "Either that, or I had better get used to the way you make this stuff because it sounds like I'll be drinking it for a while."

"Well I may test you, but I don't plan on killing you." Vance opened a small refrigerator that he had in his office and passed out some well received bottles of water. Each of them relished the pure clean liquid after the mean, bitter black java.

"Now as I was saying," Vance picked up where he left off. "You're at the stage when you have to go beyond simply memorizing. You must develop the skill of thinking. When you develop this skill you'll be able to rearrange information that you have memorized into a new perception. You've got to master your cognitive skills yourself, but we will help you as much as possible."

Bill sat back listening to Vance coach Quincy. He had heard it all before, and always enjoyed seeing his mentor excited about a new intern who had enormous potential.

"You'll learn the most from your patients if you do certain things. I'll try to show you how to do that on each patient we see. In addition, you'll be exposed to the humanistic side of medicine. Because – and you must never forget it – good medical care is the union of knowledge and caring." Vance was just starting to get fired up. He had that sparkle in his eye just like he had when he first met Bill. They spent another hour talking about Vance's philosophy of medicine.

The meeting had to end when Vance's secretary slipped into the office and quietly informed Vance that he had an important phone call.

After Quincy and Bill slipped out, the call was transferred. When Vance answered the phone, his face reflected delight. One of Vance's most famous students, Russell Hillgren was on the line. Russell studied under Vance when Russell's dad was a senator from Georgia. In fact his father, now President Hillgren, invited Vance into the political arena by having Vance testify to the Senate Health Committee, chaired by Senator Adams. Vance's testimony passionately initiated and dramatically heightened public awareness of issues inherent in the medical-legal-political-industrial complex that caused the downward spiral of medical care.

After his dad became president, Russell decided to move from Baxley, Georgia to Washington. His father wanted him close by and asked him to help with the nation's health care issues. He focused most of his attention on the rising cost of medicine. Within a few months Russell was Special Assistant to the Secretary of Health and Human Services.

For the first half-hour on the phone, Russell told Vance about activities in the White House and how his dad continued to make progress on health care issues. Finally the real reason Russell called became clear.

"My dad was impressed with your comments at the Senate Health Committee hearing a few years ago, Vance," Russell said.

"I tried to tell it like it was." Vance was saddened at the way some of his colleagues had responded. Some didn't appreciate his message and thought that he may have opened Pandora's Box by revealing the problems confronting health care. Vance believed it was critical to make the good and bad known to the public to get reform started. He argued that it was important to continue funding medical research, to eliminate the corruption in pharmaceutical houses, to look at better ways of financing the education of health care providers, to reform Medicare and HMO's, to stop wasting money in the systems and to halt the frivolously law suits. And that was only the beginning.

"My dad asked me to create a commission charged with developing a health care reform plan using the best medical experts in the country."

Vance knew where this was going. "Russell, you know that I'm not getting any younger."

"Yes, that's why I figured you'd probably have more time to work on this. After all, you've cut back some on your duties at Greystone." Russell had learned well from his father on how to challenge people to perform. "Hey, how often does the President of the United States ask for your help and consultation?"

Vance sighed deeply.

"The Country is calling you, Vance," Russell challenged.

"Ok, you've got me." Vance gave in a lot easier than Russell had anticipated. Vance added, "I want Bill with me."

"You can ask whomever you want to join you, Vance. You will be the chairman of a subcommittee of a special commission whose charge is to fix the health care system in this country. We'll be happy to pay for whatever you need." Russell was excited. "This will be your chance to spell it out, Vance. Tell us exactly what you think is needed for reform. There's one more thing, Vance."

"Yes?"

"Don't hold back this time either."

Russell was quick to get off the phone after he set a date for Vance and Bill to go to Washington D.C. to meet with the President.

Vance would soon be in the hot seat again.

He spent the rest of the afternoon trying to figure out how to tell Jennifer. She had put her foot down about adding anything to his schedule, including more traveling.

———◦———

Bill was going to stop back later to see Vance, but his arthritis was screaming at him. He still hadn't found a medicine that could even dent his pain like Jorestat-2 did. He decided to call it an early day and take it easy out at the ranch.

To Bill's surprise Connie was already home. A bigger surprise was that she had bought a bottle of Grey Goose vodka.

"So what's the occasion?" Bill asked suspiciously.

"Don't worry I just want to take down the stress a notch or two."

"Connie?"

"I said don't worry about it." Connie removed the cork. "I'm in control and you know it. So, let's just be like normal people and have a cocktail and unwind."

Bill watched her pour the drinks. They weren't stiff by any means, but he was still uneasy that she wanted a drink. "I take it you had a bad day."

Connie flavored the vodka with an olive. "I'm fed up. Every time I turn around there are personnel from insurance companies second guessing me about the medical treatment I think someone needs. I'm sick of it." Connie took a slow sip of her drink. "They eat up all my time with their damn paperwork. And on top of that the HMO administrators complain if I spend too much time with one patient. It's all about rotating those patients in and out as fast as you can."

Bill nodded knowingly. He casually gave her a soft, understanding hug. He decided it would be best to change topics.

"How was John today?" Bill asked.

John was diagnosed as having a mild autistic disorder. Luckily they could afford to have John enrolled in a special daycare for his disorder. The school was nearby where Connie worked so she could take John and pick him up without having to spend an extra couple of hours in the car.

"The school told me that he spent most of the day watching spinning wheel toys and an electric fan." Connie replied. "He also spent a lot of time sitting and rocking while he played with a rubber band. And to top it off, the supervisor told me that he has started biting other children. If it continues he might have to leave the school."

Bill turned and watched John sitting in the next room, still mildly rocking, watching cartoons.

Connie slumped back into her chair. "Why don't you check on John while I pour us another drink?"

It was one of those days. A hard day. It was a day that Bill wished he still had his Jorestat-2.

CHAPTER 5

WASHINGTON, D.C.
MARCH 2001

THE HEAVY dark gray curtains were tightly drawn. Senator Adams had, since his youth, constantly battled a skin disorder that was exacerbated by the sun. As long as he could remember he had avoided the sun. Sunlight was not permitted in Senator Adams' office. The persistent cloud of smoke from his expensive cigars drifted aimlessly throughout his office, often escaping down the hallway drawing cries of outrage. Recently, due to the mounting complaints of nearby employees, "office moles" as the senator called them, the senate maintenance department installed an air filter system so that Adams could smoke an "occasional" Cuban cigar without bothering others.

At first he hated the system because he liked to see the smoke linger. He enjoyed the sweetly acrid air. But Neil and Pamela encouraged the senator to be flexible and brought it up often enough that Senator Adams finally relinquished.

Senator Adam's office was dreary and depressing but the senator enjoyed his dimly lit refuge. A few years ago when Pamela tried to brighten the office décor with new furniture, the senator went ballistic and had the original furniture returned immediately. He liked his dull and dingy digs. Adams was sour for a week after that episode. Pamela gave up her crusade for office improvements.

The senator had called a meeting with Neil and Pamela for the late afternoon. Since it was Saturday there was very little activity going on around the Hill. That's when the senator liked to have his special strategy meetings. It was not unusual for the senator to call these meetings for Saturday or Sunday night. Of course, those meetings would often drag on into late hours. There was something about those special meetings that always charged up the senator. To him they were the essence of true politics. The senator was a backroom specialist of the best kind. A Catfish in still, dark water. Neil and Pamela were hurrying so they would not be late to the senator's meeting. Time had slipped up on them. This was Neil's weekend to stay with Pamela. One weekend every quarter was the deal they had struck. It wasn't a big price for her to pay in order to be in the middle of the senator's action. And, of course, she needed those weekends to keep herself informed of any sidebar deals that she might not have heard.

Unfortunately Neil had fallen for her. But he knew that he couldn't let his feelings interfere with business. He loathed bringing up certain evenings— like the time when Pamela escorted Triplett to a room in the senator's Mississippi mansion. Neil pushed those times out of his mind. With his distorted love for her he figured they were a team. She did those things to help them. After all, without Neil she would have nothing.

Pamela lived in an expensive condo on the edge of the Georgetown area. She liked being around the youthful energy of college students. She often found her way to the small bars that gave the area so much character and she frequently took long walks. That's why they were running late today Pamela had wanted to walk before getting ready to go to work. Late March was kind this year. The weather wasn't too bad and today was exceptionally nice. Besides, she didn't mind Neil walking along with her. In fact, it was kind of nice.

They were a little late when their driver took a straight shot down Massachusetts Avenue and then cut across some back streets to pull up in front of the Senate Office Building. Locals called it the SOB building for short. They entered Senator Adam's office. He didn't seem to notice their tardiness.

The senator was huddled over his desk. The only light on in his office was a desk light. The senator's stringy hair was in need of cutting. He always wore a suit in Washington. Didn't matter what day it was, or where he was. His collar was too tight and he looked uncomfortable. Perhaps the senator had gained a little weight. His jowls seemed flabbier these days and even his face looked ashen white and unhealthy.

The senator finally looked up at them and said, "Triplet is calling in for a conference call." He noticed that Pamela had her red hair pulled back away from her face and she looked a little bothered. Neil, of course, was all smiles. The Senator was no dummy. He could tell that Neil's heaven was her hell. "He wants an update."

"It's good timing," Neil spoke up as he sat down in a leather chair across from the senator. "I just had a conversation with Vice President Lancaster."

"Ahh yes, Mr. VP—the president's closest advisor." The senator smiled as he chewed on a cigar. He often didn't light one for hours. He would just chew on it until the spit made it too soggy to ignite. "And just what does the vice president say now?"

"He said that President Hillgren is making a special push on health care." Neil was proud of his inside line to the vice president.

Several years ago Neil knew that Joe Lancaster, then a senator, was going to be a very big player in Washington. After all Joe Lancaster had been, over the last decade, responsible for the economic strategy of the Democrats. Neil had made a number of thoroughly calculated investments for the future. Some of them ended up paying off. The decision he made many years ago to gain the indebtedness of Lancaster turned out to be one of his smoothest accomplishments.

Neil waited patiently for his plan to unfold. He had called it, "operation smash down". He had picked a night when Joe Lancaster attended a black tie party at an estate on the Potomac about twenty miles outside of Washington. Everyone who was anyone was there, including Neil and Pamela.

Lancaster preferred to do his own driving. He hated limos and chose instead a black Crown Victoria. His wife, the down to earth type, never cared about limos either. Neil counted on Lancaster's driving that evening. Just by luck, it was a moonless night and the visibility was terrible. Everything that unfolded that evening was finely choreographed. Neil had checked the details a thousand times. Lancaster had only been going about fifteen miles an hour over the speed limit. About forty-five or fifty. He was using his yellow lights in the dense fog. They were much better for vision in his opinion. He was taking a sharp curve when it happened. Lancaster saw the single headlight directly in front of his car. The car screeched as he slammed on the brakes. He lost control of the car and it swerved across the median. There was nothing he could do as he skidded sideways in an attempt to stop. The motorcycle slid across the pavement trying to avoid the impending head-on collision. The motorcycle dropped flat down onto the pavement, leaving a trail of sparks and fire. Smoke curled. Lancaster's air bag exploded as he hit the concrete divider cutting off his visual field. He heard the motorcycle sliding by as it barely missed his car and splashed into the Potomac River.

Neil's limo was the first to arrive at the scene. One of his bodyguards helped Lancaster get out of his car. He was obviously struggling to regain his composure. The other bodyguard chucked his coat and shoes and dove bravely into the water in a desperate effort to retrieve the driver of the motorcycle. Again and again he surfaced and dove, but it was hopeless. Neil had one of his men drive the visibly shaken Lancaster and his wife back to the Lancaster's home, while he stayed back to explain to the police what had happened. He had assured Lancaster that he would "take care of it for him." Of course, Neil's story to the police was a sham. According to Neil's story, it was the driver of his limo who nearly hit a dog and just missed the motorcycle. Joe Lancaster's name or his car were never even mentioned.

The scenario had been a production that the best movie producer would have been proud of. Neil had hired the best for this job. Everything was planned to the second and it came off perfectly. Lancaster believed it all. But it was all a trick, a sleight of hand. The motorcyclist was an expert for this sort of stunt and had simply gotten into a waiting boat after he hit the river. No wonder the body wasn't found. The paper covered the story just as Neil described it. There were no charges. Of course, that little favor had Joe Lancaster, the future vice president, squarely in Neil's debt.

"Go on." The senator leaned back in his chair pulling out the mangled cigar that he had been chewing and sucking on for at least the last hour. He opened his pocket-knife and cut off the mangled part. After tossing away the two inches or so of wet, gooey tobacco, the senator stuck the cigar back in his mouth and began chewing again. "I'm assuming you got the entire scoop."

Neil didn't hesitate. "It sounds like Hillgren is going to have a commission to recommend changes for the health care system. He has already lined up the press to make a big campaign out of it all. He plans on sharing the limelight with a dozen senators."

"Bipartisan, of course?" the senator asked.

"Yes sir."

"Any of them on my health care committee?" The senator asked.

"A few."

Senator Adams smiled.

Neil emphasized. "He's certainly trying to make this the focus of his presidency. I think his legacy will be made or broken on this issue."

"And just who is heading this up for him?"

"That's the beauty of it all, Senator." It was times like this that Neil was proud of his political savvy. "The vice president is getting a special appointment by the president to head this up."

The senator didn't say anything. He just sat there with a big catfish grin and a far away look in his eyes. Three minutes passed before the phone rang abruptly and broke the silence. It was a speaker-phone so several people could listen and respond.

Senator Adams let the phone ring four times before using his index finger to press the speaker button. He gave a terse, "Hello."

Triplett didn't beat around the bush. "Let's get down to business." His tone reflected his impatience. "What's Hillgren up to now?"

Neil gave a quick recap of what he told the senator.

Triplett interrupted. "And I assume the vice president will be very receptive of our efforts?"

Neil reassured Triplett that vice president Lancaster was in their pocket. So were a few of the commission members. In the end Triplett would carry the day. Nothing much would change. The drug and instrument profit game would, with a little political finesse, stay essentially the same.

"Are you going to make sure that we don't have any damaging testimony this time?" Triplett remembered all too well Vance Connelly's presentation to Senator Adams' subcommittee on health.

Triplett enjoyed slipping that little reminder into the conversation. The senator deserved it.

"We already know who is heading up the physician team and will be reporting to the commission." The senator tossed his chewed up, soggy nub of a cigar into the trashcan. Like a boxer getting a second shot at a title fight, he boasted, "I'm ready this time."

"You'd better be." Triplett warned. "Who does Hillgren want?"

"He wants Vance Connelly." Neil said in a matter of fact tone.

"Connelly again." Triplett was indeed enjoying this. "Do you have a plan?"

"We're in the midst of creating one." Neil replied.

"According to the vice president," Neil plugged his relationship with vice president Lancaster whenever he had the opportunity, "Connelly was approached unofficially by the president's son."

"Really?" Triplett recalled that the president's son was a physician. "Maybe we should interact with Hillgren's son."

No one responded.

Triplett decided to share his idea. "You know, make a splash in the news. Have some patient he's treated back in Georgia nail him with a malpractice suit. We could drum up some kind of inappropriate sexual contact. The press loves that kind of stuff."

Pamela stood up and said. "Could work." She walked closer to the speakerphone. "But, what we really need is the information that Connelly's team will put together. We need to be able to control and manipulate the information they use."

"Couldn't we just remove Connelly as a player?" Triplett asked.

"That could get messy real quick. Besides the president would just pick someone else and tighten the security. No, it's better to control the preparation of the report."

They could hear Triplett give a soft chuckle of agreement. "I believe you're a natural at this Pamela."

"Some say so." Pamela responded warmly.

Neil hated how her eyes brightened and her voice when she talked to Triplett.

"So what's your plan?" Triplett asked.

The senator took over the conversation. "I thought we'd plant somebody inside Connelly's team."

"And just how are you going to do that?" Triplett wanted the details.

"Well," the senator smiled knowing that Triplett would appreciate his idea. "These days every team has to have a computer whiz."

Triplett was intrigued. "Go on."

"So, I had Neil here ask a little favor from the vice president."

Neil jumped into the conversation. "I asked the vice president if he would give a friend of mine the lead job with Computer Information Systems for Connelly's subcommittee."

"So who did you plant?" Triplett was starting to picture the plan.

"Who else?" Pamela spoke up, "Won't I be a prefect CIS coordinator?"

Triplett laughed suggestively. "You certainly have excellent qualifications."

Pamela had that smile on her face again that Neil hated so much. She never looked that way when he spoke to her.

"I'm going down to Atlanta to work directly with Connelly's team." Pamela explained. "I'll bounce back and forth between Washington and Atlanta for a while."

"I was just thinking." Triplett changed the tone of his voice again. "I just bought a place recently in Atlanta."

Pamela half-laughed knowing where this was heading.

Triplett believed in luxury. Boats. Cars. And houses. Actually Triplett owned several luxury condos. Besides the one in Ponte Vera, he also had one in New York, San Francisco and Atlanta. Each of them was worth several million dollars.

Pamela's right eyebrow arched. "So, are you going to show it to me?"

"Absolutely." Triplett added softly. "I think I'll plan on spending my spring in Atlanta."

Neil stood up and approached the desk. He had a wild stare in his eyes. "Excuse me," he interrupted their little flirt game, "let's concentrate on the job at hand."

The senator could see the pain in Neil's face. The clinched jaw. The narrowing of the eyes. Pain through and through. And over what? Pamela. Triplett didn't like the sharp tone in Neil's voice. "I don't believe that I asked for your input Neil."

Neil knew that Triplett was no one to make mad. It was time for Neil to back down. He wanted to tell Triplett where to go but instead he calmly backed away from the desk. Silently he turned away. He could feel Pamela eyeing him as he walked toward the exit. With the click of the office door, Pamela and the senator were left behind to deal with Triplett.

The senator was the first to speak up. "I believe Neil suddenly had a bit of a sour stomach. You'll have to forgive him for having to leave."

It was one of the few times the senator had ever made an excuse for Neal. It certainly wasn't in the senator's character to smooth over anyone's pitfalls. He wasn't really sure why he did so this time, but Neil had always watched the senators' back and maybe the senator felt he owed him a favor.

The truth was that Triplett disliked Neil. "What is his role going to be anyway?"

Triplett never liked to have anyone involved with his plans if he or she was not needed. Simple and essential roles were all he ever liked.

"He's a mastermind when it comes to this stuff and besides who else can control the vice president?" Pamela challenged.

The senator was pleased to see Pamela remind Triplett of the political need for all of them.

"Good point." Triplett never said good-bye at the end of a conversation. "I expect to hear from you next week." He hung up.

Their conference call was over.

The senator and Pamela called out for lunch and continued discussing their plans.

CHAPTER 6

ATLANTA, GEORGIA
APRIL 2001

AT 6:10 a.m. Greystone University Hospital was entirely different than during the usual clamor of daily activity. It was almost void of people and conversation. Even the hospital phones were taking a rest. Although Quincy was by no means a morning person, he did find himself enjoying the crack of dawn shift that Vance had established for him at the hospital. He found himself getting up with more energy every day. He had created a little game of counting the number of times he could beat Vance to their morning meeting. Roughly, Vance was ahead by a dozen or so. But today was Quincy's victory. Chalk one up for the new kid.

Quincy watched Vance amble down the hallway toward his office. Vance was speaking to the orderlies and they warmly reciprocated his good will. He heard Vance talking to a Vietnamese lady who worked for the janitorial service. Vance spent ten minutes talking to her about her five children.

Almost everyone said good morning to Vance as he roamed the halls. Vance loved seeing each of them. He was not physically strong, but his spirit was powerful. He was a man who understood himself and his mission in life. Quincy knew that and planned to learn all he could from Vance.

Silently Vance pulled out his keys to his office door, while Quincy stood next to him, a big grin on his face. Vance knew all about Quincy's grin. Quincy always grinned when he beat Vance to the office.

He figured that he had chalked up another one on the chief. At least he did until Vance opened the door slowly and strolled into his office. That's when Quincy noticed that Vance didn't turn on his office lights. They were already on. Quincy was also hit by the smell of coffee. Vance pulled out another cup and waived it toward Quincy. "Care for an eye opener?"

Quincy's smile disappeared as he realized that Vance had already been in his office writing an article. Apparently Vance had just taken a break to wander through the halls and see his friends.

Quincy visualized a mental subtraction from his score board and chalked one up for Vance instead. Suddenly Quincy's morning wasn't quite as special as it was a moment ago when he thought he had beaten Vance to the hospital.

Vance handed Quincy his coffee and then led him over to his round table desk. Quincy always sat in the same place. The table held four, plus Vance's bigger chair. Quincy liked to sit at an angle to Vance, about two chairs away on Vance's left side. He watched as Vance leaned back into his chair, a reflective look in his eyes.

"I've been observing you for some time now, Quincy."

Quincy was in the middle of a sip of coffee and froze. "And?"

"I think you're going to be an exceptional doctor, someday."

Quincy could tell that was just the opener. Vance was setting the stage for something that Quincy needed to understand before he could become a better physician.

"But, you've got to go to the next level." Vance's eyes were penetrating. "I think you know what I mean."

"Actually," Quincy was dumbfounded, "I don't have a clue."

Quincy decided that he wouldn't be the one to break the eye contact. He knew this was a challenge. Not an overt challenge, but a challenge nonetheless. No matter what Vance had to say Quincy felt he had to maintain his friendly stare. He decided to listen and not defend.

"You have a tendency to cruise at a comfortable pace when you should be leading the pack."

"I maintained a straight A average during med school."

"That's my point." Vance countered. "You're creating a ceiling for yourself. You're doing just enough to prove that you're one of the best."

Vance took another sip of coffee, but never lost the eye contact. "For you to go to the next level, you've got to throw away the goals that other people give you. You have to feel the excitement within you when you are achieving what you know you can achieve." Vance put down his coffee mug and leaned forward. "You've felt it at different points in your life I'm sure. You've felt the adrenaline pumping through your system when you're on to something that you know your soul is telling you to do. The sweat and, yes, the agony of stretching yourself. That's the next level, stretching yourself."

"Is that why you write so much?" Quincy wanted the attention off of himself.

"Yes, it drives me. I have the feeling that my work is not yet complete. Perhaps, someday. But, not yet. I have a mission and something tells me when I'm on the right path. I know who I am and what I stand for in this world."

Quincy nodded. Slowly he looked down at his hands. Young, strong and untested.

"My time is almost over Quincy. But you're just coming up to bat." Vance's tone deepened. "How you deal with it now will either set you free and keep you playing the game, or just look good on paper."

Quincy nodded. He wanted to say something, but the words were lost.

Vance continued. "I want you to reach for it. Retrieve a memory or create a new idea. But—here is the catch—whatever you do, it must be uniquely yours."

Now they were on a level playing field. They had established an honest relationship. They understood each other.

From now on their relationship would be different. There was no hiding now for Quincy.

A soft knock at the door broke the silent spell that Vance had wrapped so neatly around Quincy. It was Bill. He sensed that the two were locked into something serious, something more than just medicine. Yet, he also sensed that this was a good point for an interruption.

"Excuse me." Bill said with caution in case he'd misjudged his timing. He wanted to slip into the conversation slowly. "Have you read the paper this morning?"

Bill showed the headlines detailing President Hillgren's official announcement that Vice President Joe Lancaster would be the medical reform czar.

Bill started to size up the situation, "How long before the vice president calls us up to Washington?"

Vance still had the newspaper in his hand. "I imagine in the next week or so he'll want to get all the formalities out of the way and ask us to start compiling a strategy."

Quincy sat up. "Are you gonna do this?"

Vance pointed out a sentence in the paper that explained Vance's role.

Quincy knew the president's son had been one of Vance's students. And he also knew immediately what he wanted to do and for the first time in a long while he acted on impulse. He knew that this wasn't the time to be stealthy. "I want in."

Vance didn't reply. He simply continued to read the paper, noticing that some of the print had rubbed off on the tips of his fingers.

Quincy repeated. "I don't know how I can be of help yet, but I want to be on your team."

Vance pulled a handkerchief out of his pocket and started to rub the print off his fingers.

"Dr. Connelly," Quincy's raised his voice noticeably, "I really want a chance to work on this."

Vance gave Bill a quick glance and then studied Quincy for a moment. "What about your internship and residency?"

Quincy had no reservations. "I'm sure you can find someone to fill my slot until this is over."

Vance had already pictured Quincy wanting to be part of the team. Things were starting to take shape.

"The first thing I want to do is tell you both what I know about the vice president." Vance was already picking up his pace and his thoughts were racing. Vance shuffled the paper to the side. "Were you aware that his uncle, Robert Lancaster, died here in this hospital?"

Quincy face reflected his surprise. "When?"

"Back in 1952 shortly after I first began working at the hospital."

Bill looked over at Quincy. "Vance not only started his career off with a drama, but he also found his wife, Jennifer, in the midst of it all."

Vance smiled at the memory. "She was Miss Eden at that time. And, yes, I met her on the cardiology ward. She was a nurse."

Earlier Quincy had noticed a small black and white picture of Connelly with a beautiful woman. The picture hung on the wall with a half dozen other photographs of that period.

"I've only told a handful of people this story." Vance was on the fence about telling it now but he decided to let it rip.

Quincy and Bill quickly settled back into their chairs. They sat motionless, intently listening.

"Like I said, it took place back in 1952." Vance closed his eyes as he recalled the details of the story. "It was October 1952 to be exact."

"That was before I was even born." Quincy couldn't help but toss in his comment.

Vance smiled at Quincy's little jab. "Yes, Quincy, lots of things happened before you were born." Still keeping his eyes closed, Vance let his mind slide into a different era.

CHAPTER 7

ATLANTA, GEORGIA
OCTOBER 1952

IT WAS 12:30 a.m. when Jennifer Eden screamed for the first time in her adult life. There was no pain in her scream, yet she was doubled over, clutching her elbows as she backed out of room 620 on the East wing of Greystone University Hospital. Her face was ashen and her lips were twisted into a horrible grimace. Her gray eyes were wide, staring fixedly with disbelief. It wasn't a scream of physical pain at all nor was it a scream of anger. There was an eerie darkness about her scream. A soul-shocked sound that echoed down the hallway with such force that it stunned her co-workers into total silence and paralysis before they started moving toward the noise.

Everything had started as a typical run of the mill night. A cold front with a light drizzle of rain peppered the city. Atlanta was quiet and sedate. Jennifer's drive down to the hospital was, at 10:30 p.m., clear of most traffic. Jennifer was fifteen minutes early for the graveyard shift. She was always at least fifteen minutes early for work, probably because she never thought of nursing as just another job. No one could remember a single time that Jennifer was late or called in for sick leave, at least not in the two years since she had signed on at Greystone University Hospital. Although Jennifer was only in her late twenties, she was respected for her nursing talent.

Her style was typically low-key, always in control, professional. Her auburn hair was shoulder length and her cream-colored skin was beautiful. Her high cheek bones gave her the classic model image. Her character was never questioned and she carried a good sense of humor. More than one of the young, male, medical house officers had dreamed about her. Few had the courage to approach her. And all of them soon learned that she never mixed business with pleasure.

She was a private person. At the center of Jennifer's existence was her focus on control. It wasn't the selfish control of others that Jennifer sought, but rather, her sense of control from within. It was like a veteran athlete internally coordinating each moment into action.

That's why it was so alarming for Jennifer's cohorts to see her out of control with such terror in her eyes. They rushed to her as she gasped for a breath. "It's Robert." Her body vibrated visibly. Her hands were balled tight making white-knuckled fists. "My God, it's Robert."

A small huddle of nurses gathered around Jennifer instantly. Several of the patients drifted into the hallway. Some cracked the doors of their room. Jennifer felt the presence of a dozen pair of anxious eyes.

"What is it, darlin'?" A short older nurse with gray streaks in her hair asked in her usual soft southern drawl. She was holding Jennifer by the arm and gently escorting her toward a chair.

Jennifer squeezed the old nurse's arm tighter.

"Don't be gettin' all worked up now." The old nurse felt as if she were swimming up stream. Jennifer was near panic.

Jennifer stopped short of the chair and paused to regain her breathing. She felt a little dizzy, but the presence of the old nurse, coupled with her long history of dealing with medical emergencies, Jennifer's reflex for control clicked into action. She steadied herself.

The color in Jennifer's face was slowly returning, "Call the emergency room to send some doctors to the driveway." Jennifer's lips trembled as she spoke. " Robert...Mr. Lancaster jumped out of the window."

"Jumped!"

"Yes, he's... He's got to be..." Jennifer tagged on a follow-up command. "Also," she looked the old nurse in the eye, "I want you to call security and tell them that we need help."

Quietly and efficiently the other nurses guided patients back into their rooms.

The shallow tide of soft murmurs slowly dissipated as the hallway was cleared. Eyes still peered from the doorways. Within minutes a security guard dressed in gray was running down the hallway. He was a young slender man with blonde hair and a standard issue pistol strapped to his hip.

The guard stopped a few feet from Jennifer. "What's going on?"

Jennifer took the time to sit down. "You had better seal off that room." She pointed to room 620 then rubbed the back of her slender neck, "A patient jumped out of the window."

The guard shouted over to the nurse's station. "Call the security office and report a Code 28... that's Code 28 on 6E." Code 28 was the standard procedure for calling the police and getting more security immediately into the area. Code 28 had never been used at Greystone before this evening. He returned to Jennifer. "Ok, why don't you tell me what happened."

Jennifer was still collecting herself.

"Miss Eden, please," the guard persisted, "I need to know what happened up here."

Jennifer held up her hand. "Just a minute." She looked back at the old nurse. "Get in touch with Dr. Wassermann, he's the attending physician."

"Anything else?" The old nurse asked.

"Yes," Jennifer inhaled deeply, "tell Dr. Wassermann to call the Chief."

Connelly had recently been appointed the Chief of Medicine at

Greystone. He was a young man in his early thirties, tall and slender, with wavy brown hair. He wore horn-rimmed glasses that gave him an intellectual look. He was perhaps the youngest chief of medicine in the country. And he was definitely a hands-on type of boss. Everything had to go through Connelly.

"Mam," the guard edged closer, "the doctors on duty just announced that Robert Lancaster is dead."

Jennifer nodded.

"Now, tell me, what happened up here?" the guard carefully pressed, "Did you see him jump?"

Before Jennifer could reply, a small force of three men in blue uniforms and one man in a dark gray tweed coat with light gray pants turned the corner of the hallway. They were the police responding to the Code 28.

Their pace was brisk and their faces determined. The man in the tweed coat carried a small walkie-talkie and barked his orders.

With a quick flip of a wallet he showed his badge. "I'm Lieutenant Lee, Cameron Lee."

The security guard looked at his watch, "Good response time, Lieutenant."

Cameron ignored the young guard's comment and looked down at Jennifer. "Were you the nurse on duty?"

"Yes."

The guard was anxious to interrupt, "Looks like a patient jumped out of the window."

Cameron glanced at the young guard and lifted his eyebrows as if to ask, "Aren't you a regular Sherlock Holmes?" Cameron planted his gaze on the young man's eyes, "Listen, son, let me get my own information." Cameron never did like rent-a-cops. They were so protective of the organization that paid them that they'd run interference instead of providing critical information. He had learned long ago that the best thing to do was get them out from underfoot.

The security guard backed away as Cameron got up closer into his face. "Son," Cameron's breath smelled of old coffee and stale tobacco, "why don't you go out and watch the parking lot?"

Cameron's forty-five year old face resembled a determined bulldog with one slightly cocked eye. No one ever knew when he was actually looking at them unless he squared off with them. Texas born, he was not known for his diplomacy. He liked unfiltered Camels, cheap beer, and spicy Mexican food. His chest was stout, but his waist was under control. He maintained a strong set of biceps. Sporting a crew cut, he figured that he wasn't too bad looking for a beat up old fighter.

The guard fought back. "As part of the security of this hospital I should be in on this investigation…"

Looking as if he had had enough, Cameron replied sternly. "Good day, son."

Cameron eased a little distance from the guard as the young man reluctantly turned and began a long lanky stroll down the hallway.

"Cameron." one of the officers stood in the doorway of room 620, "You want to see the room?"

Cameron nodded and went to scan the darkened room. He waited for his eyes to adjust, stepped farther into the room, paused and closed the door.

The room had an odor of bleach.

It was dark, but not pitch black. A crack of light at the bottom of the doorway gave just enough illumination in the room to see the outline of the furniture. The bed dominated the room. One chair. A small table.

Cameron flipped on the fluorescent light. Nothing seemed out of place. The bed sheets were ruffled with no overt sign of disturbance. A slight breeze eased into the room from the open window. Cameron walked across the room and studied it. There were actually two windows, one on top of the other. Each windowpane was approximately three feet wide and three feet tall. The top window was stationary. Originally, the bottom window could slide up and down on its tracks. In the old days, before air conditioning, the window was opened for fresh air, and then a high-ranking politician in Washington used the window of his hospital room to say good-bye to this world. His famous leap forced many hospitals to start bolting their windows shut. Thank God air conditioning was available. Cameron noticed that the bolts to the lower window had been removed. The window was raised and the bolts were on the floor. There was dust on the windowsill. He realized that the paint covering the bolts was old and must have been reduced to powder when the bolts were removed. As he studied the scene the light caught something in the powder. A small speck of material no bigger than the size of a pinhead glittered. Maybe it was glass, but there was no sign of broken glass anywhere and nothing else glittered. He backed slowly away and returned to the hallway.

"Should I guard it now?" The officer standing by the door asked.

"Yes, I don't want anyone to enter this room. Except for the investigators." Cameron wrote down a message for the officer to give the investigators. *Be sure to seal the bolts and the dust around the windowsill and on the floor.* Maybe the guys in investigations could sift something out of the mess.

Cameron saw a doctor standing by Jennifer. He walked over authoritatively. "Do you have something to do with this?"

"Indirectly, yes, I do." The man spoke confidently.

"And you are?" Cameron asked.

"My name is Doctor Wassermann...Doctor Harold E. Wassermann."

"Ok, Doctor Harold E. Wassermann, what's your role in this?"

At first sight Cameron didn't care for this man. He was the type that had the Doctor God syndrome written all over his forehead. Probably a chess player who drank single malt Scotch and read the Sunday paper front to back except for the sports page. Cameron put a lot of stock in his first impression of a person. He didn't like Wassermann. He didn't care for the perfectly styled dark hair with the pedantic cast to his ocean gray eyes and a weak chin to boot. No, this guy was not anybody Cameron would go down to a bar with and cut loose for the evening.

"To answer your question, Lieutenant," Wassermann seemed impatient. "I was called down here. I was Mr. Lancaster's physician."

Cameron remained quiet as he continued to size this man up.

"I also called our Chief of Medicine, Dr. Connelly." Wassermann explained.

Cameron muttered something about red tape and then looked hard at Wassermann. "So when does your boss show up?" Cameron emphasized the word "boss" because he had a hunch that it would irritate a man like Wassermann.

"Dr. Connelly," Wassermann returned Cameron's volley, "should be here any minute."

Cameron looked at his watch. It was nearly 1:00 a.m. Turning around, Cameron looked for an office that he could confiscate for the evening. It was definitely going to be an all nighter. A five or six cup night. "Is there a room around here that we can use to sort this out?"

Jennifer pointed to a small staff room next to the nurses' station, a convenient place for the nurses to have their report when they changed shifts. Cameron had just taken a seat at the table when Vance walked into the room.

Wassermann remained standing and silent. Jennifer was seated at the table but was somewhat boxed off by Cameron. She extended a brief nod and Connelly returned it.

It was Cameron's turn. He stood up Texas tall and shook Connelly's hand. Connelly's grip was surprisingly strong. His brown eyes were magnified by his glasses and his deep stare never wavered from Cameron. Cameron liked that in a person. There was something genuine about Vance. Perhaps, just perhaps, here was a man who valued his profession and his name. At least, that was Cameron's first impression.

After they exchanged a brief introduction, Cameron asked. "I assume that Wassermann briefed you over the phone?"

Vance nodded as he sat up straight in his chair and crossed his arms comfortably in front of his chest.

Cameron pulled out a small note pad, "Who can give me a little background on Lancaster?"

Wassermann spoke up. "I've been his physician for the last year."

Cameron nodded for him to start.

"His family lives in Boston." Wassermann didn't need to look at his notes for that part. "The Lancaster's are known for their banking business throughout the country. From what I understand Robert Lancaster was running the southeast region for his family."

Cameron had heard the name, he remembered a young Lancaster from Boston who was elected to US Congress. Wasserman continued. "Here is his chart with my medical notes." He passed the chart over to Cameron.

> Patient: Robert Lancaster
> Date: October 13, 1952
>
> The patient checked into the emergency room complaining of chest discomfort. His recent onset of angina pectoris may have been triggered by the excessive stress over a business deal. The patient is a heavy smoker. During the patient interview the patient reported a history of mood swings. At the time of the medical exam the patient appeared to be emotionally agitated.
>
> The physical examination was normal except for the blood pressure which was 170/90. His electrocardiogram was normal.
>
> The patient was given nitroglycerin to take if he had any chest pain. An ECG will be recorded during the time the patient is having an episode of chest pain. A light sedative will be prescribed for sleeping.

"I'm not sure if I know what some of this means," Cameron jotted down a few things and returned the chart to Wasserman. "But I do get the general picture."

Cameron tapped his pen on his notepad as he continued to question Wasserman. "Why do you think he was agitated?"

"He told me that he was one week away from signing the final agreement of the biggest deal in his life." Wassermann cleared his throat. "I remember him saying that he was up at all hours trying to make this deal happen."

"I'm surprised he stopped everything and came into the hospital." Cameron put down his pencil and rubbed his hands together. "He sounds like the type that gets obsessed with his work."

"Lieutenant," Wasserman's weak chin was sticking out a bit, "I'm sure Lancaster had enough money so that he valued his health over another deal."

Cameron leaned toward Wassermann, "You know that for a fact?"

"Well, the man talked to me about his new expensive home in Buckhead. A six bedroom home. He also had a condominium in Charleston and made trips overseas that sounded exotic."

Cameron took in what Wasserman reported and then changed the topic. "How much sedative did he get?"

"He received enough to calm him down." Wassermann seemed irritated by the questions.

"He could still function then?"

"Yes." Wassermann looked at his watch. "Lieutenant, it's almost 1:30 in the morning. I need to get in touch with Mrs. Lancaster and tell her about her husband. She has a right to know what's happened."

Cameron looked at the others in the room before replying. "Yes, of course. I've gathered enough background information for now. I want to focus on what happened tonight." Cameron stood up and opened the door and dismissed Wassermann.

Cameron made the arrangements with one of his fellow officers to accompany Wasserman and explain what had happened to Lancaster's wife. He then went over the details of the evening with Jennifer. Vance remained for the duration of the interview as Cameron gathered enough notes for his first impression. The meeting broke up around 7:00 a.m. just in time for Jennifer to explain it all to the next shift of nurses. Cameron continued to survey the entire area and waited for Jennifer to finish her report.

Jennifer was exhausted. She must have told her story to Cameron at least three times. How she was making her rounds. How surprised she was when she entered Robert Lancaster's room and found an empty bed. The light was off in the bathroom. No noise. The soft, jarring, gale of cold wind forced her to notice the open window. The muscles of her jaw, neck and shoulders tightened as she edged her way to the window and peered outside. The barely visible body of Robert Lancaster was near the driveway. His body almost concealed by a row of large bushes. Yes, it was a memory that would be forever etched in her mind.

Cameron walked Jennifer to her car. There was a light haze of dampness. "Are you certain that no one entered that room after you discovered what happened?"

"Positive."

"Can you get me a list of everyone that saw Mr. Lancaster from the time that he arrived at his room?"

"That may be impossible."

"Don't the nurses keep records?"

Jennifer sighed heavily. "Our nurses are the best, but they can't keep up with everyone who visits a patient."

"How about his family? Could somebody at least tell me if his wife came over to see him?"

"Maybe."

"What about during your shift?"

"Well," Jennifer continued to talk as she opened her handbag and stirred around for the keys to her car, "he did leave his room once," she recalled. "Yes, Dr. Wasserman had ordered an x-ray film of his chest.

So I had a nurse's aid take Mr. Lancaster down to the x-ray department in a wheelchair around 11:15 p.m. I suspect he saw people there, at least he saw the x-ray technicians for sure."

Cameron pulled out his little note pad and recorded what Jennifer told him. He watched as she unlocked and opened the door of her blue Ford. "Tell me, Miss Eden, has the hospital ever had a problem like this before?"

"No, not that I know of."

Cameron told her that he would be in touch soon. He watched as she drove off, and then took his time walking back to the hospital. He wanted to see where Lancaster had landed. The body and surroundings were photographed by the police before the body was removed. A few reporters were still lingering around the scene trying to get information from Vance. A couple of flashes of light let Cameron know that his picture would make the next edition of the *Constitution*. The police kept the reporters back behind a predetermined line. When Cameron approached Vance some reporters started shouting questions at the two of them.

"Any idea as to why he jumped, Lieutenant?"

Cameron smiled as he gave a pat answer. "Wait till we finish our investigation boys."

"Doctor Connelly, do you think it was a suicide?" An aggressive reporter barked as he pressed closer.

"No comment." Vance replied simply.

"Lieutenant, you think there could be foul play involved?" The same reporter demanded.

"Our investigation has not been concluded at this time." Cameron repeated.

Others scrambled to ask questions but Cameron turned his back to the reporters and walked toward the hospital entrance. He turned back just in time to see Vance making his way toward the parking lot.

This had all the signs of a long day after a long sleepless night. As Cameron started to enter the elevator to go back to the sixth floor, the old nurse who had been around the crime scene walked out.

Cameron was fast to step away from the elevator. "Ma'm, what was the first thing you heard tonight?"

"All I heard was Jennifer's scream." The old nurse recalled.

"That's it? A scream? No commotion beforehand?"

"Just a scream." The old nurse lifted her head and looked at Cameron's face. "She screamed and then I remember her saying the name Robert."

The ride up in the elevator gave Cameron just enough time to mull over the old nurse's comments. Something about it was gnawing at Cameron. Why would Jennifer, a highly trained professional, scream Lancaster's first name? Robert Lancaster had only been there a few hours.

When the elevator opened Cameron marched back to room 620. A policeman was positioned next to the entrance. Cameron opened the door and walked over to check the window again. Once more Cameron got that funny feeling that something just wasn't quite right.

Vance Connelly had his usual morning report at 7:00 a.m. The house officers presented him a brief account of all the new patients admitted to the hospital during the preceding 24 hours. Morning report was held in the conference room next to Vance's office. The Robert Lancaster case would dominate the morning.

Morning report was usually limited to Connelly and the house officers but Connelly had decided to ask Wassermann to discuss the unfortunate recent turn of events. The medical aspects of the Lancaster case made for a good presentation. Vance thought it would be wise to have Cameron there as well. This way the doors of communication could be opened.

At the end of the house officer's presentation Wassermann's eyes had a far off look as he reported. "I'm afraid that I underestimated one of his problems." Wasserman looked around the room. "I'm afraid that I didn't realize the extent of his depression."

One of the young male interns challenged Wasserman. "In fact, in your notes you mentioned that he seemed somewhat agitated."

"Yes," Wassermann gave a heavy sigh. "Clearly, the diagnosis of depression is difficult." He second-guessed himself. "I suspect he was depressed because most patients who commit suicide are depressed."

"Something doesn't fit here." Vance had that squint in his eye. "I believe depressed people often leave a suicide note and to my knowledge the police haven't found one."

A hush dominated the room.

Only the hissing noise of the air vents could be heard.

Vance waited for comments, but there were none. He ended the conference by saying, "So far, we don't know why this tragedy occurred. We'll need to work with the police to get to the bottom of this case." Vance introduced Cameron to the group as the man in charge of the investigation.

After the meeting when the others filed out, Vance waited for Cameron to make his way to the front.

"I've always known that medicine and detective work were a lot alike." Cameron stated as he followed Vance toward his office.

Vance agreed. "People sometimes think of medicine as a science, but there is a lot more art to it than science. I take it that you have to feel your way through things at times."

Cameron nodded.

"And what sort of questions do you ask to get to the bottom of a situation like this?" Vance asked curiously.

"Usually questions about motive."

"Like greed and anger?"

Cameron added. "Along with fear, and lust, or just plain meanness."

"Figuring out the motive. Now that could be tricky."

"Absolutely. Human desire is endless."

"I suppose the science comes into play after you gather some evidence, like fingerprints." Vance had heard a lot about the new technology of criminology. "No telling where crime investigation will be by the end of the fifties."

Vance posed the question. "So you don't think it was suicide?"

"Can't prove it, but something isn't right."

Vance's forehead wrinkled deeply.

Cameron stood up and started to walk with Vance toward his office. "Lancaster was a man who was making a lot of money, very rich."

"And he was making enough to give someone else a motive." Vance replied.

"I believe so."

"So you can't discount greed."

"Nope."

Vance opened the door of his office and led the way for Cameron.

Cameron continued, "Well, he was about to close a big deal, so if it was greed, well, somebody in the deal might have had a lot to lose."

The light in Vance's office was bright but the color of the walls made it seem restful.

"Just doesn't add up." Cameron face revealed his confusion.

Vance sat back into his office chair. "Lieutenant, let's lay our cards on the table. Do you really believe that Lancaster was murdered?"

Cameron didn't want to give a fast reply when there was no evidence, but still as he exhaled heavily he said, "Yes, I do."

"And your first hunch is that greed was involved?"

Cameron rubbed the back of his neck. "No, not really, but a motive usually surfaces sooner or later."

Vance's secretary gave a light tap on the door before entering the room. She was a middle-aged woman who always had a friendly smile. She reminded Vance not to forget that he had an appointment with the president of the university in twenty minutes. The president wanted to be fully informed before the press hounds nipped at his heels.

Vance gathered his notes for his meeting. "Can I assure him that until there is clear evidence nothing will be released to the press?"

Cameron agreed.

"And," Cameron stood up casually, "I assume that I can count on your support throughout my investigation."

Vance finished gathering his notes before replying. "In other words you need an inside ally that will tell you everything we find out?"

With a half grin and a single nod, Cameron punctuated the point.

"How about if the information flows both ways?"

"Doctor Connelly," Cameron's grin widened, "are you sure that you're not part lawyer?"

They shook hands. The handshake wasn't casual, nor did it signify friendship. It was a handshake of mutual respect and honor.

His secretary gave another light knock on the door to remind Vance of the time.

There was nothing in the morning paper about Robert Lancaster because the morning Constitution had long ago been tossed onto the streets. The radio and TV stations, however, were having their usual field day over the tragedy. The reporters had plenty of time to gather incidentals about Robert Lancaster's life before the noon broadcast. They described him as a handsome businessman with a Scandinavian heritage. Of course, the newspaper guys were crawling everywhere at Greystone. Vance knew that tomorrow's paper would show photographs of Lancaster and the scene where he fell as well as photographs of Greystone University Hospital.

CHAPTER 8

ATLANTA, GEORGIA
MAY 2001

IT WAS the first time Pamela had ever set foot in Buckhead, the original "place to be seen" suburb of Atlanta, referred to as "Hotlanta." Buckhead was known for its fine restaurants and grandiose homes, but also for its abundance of exclusive upscale singles bars. Lots of old and new money mixed and mingled. Pamela was there to get a feel for the city. Of course, she had plans to meet with Triplett. He was staying at his penthouse condo on Peachtree Street. In character, he lavished himself with the finer things of an expensive life style.

Pamela didn't talk directly with Triplett to set up this trip. He was always too busy or was out of his office. Triplett's secretary arranged the meeting. Pamela was given instructions to be at his hotel room by noon. She hated it when she was given indirect, impersonal orders, let alone orders from someone's secretary. But, this was clearly a command performance. She didn't even get a phone call. Instead, the secretary sent an impersonal e-mail that stated the time, place and agenda for their meeting.

It was 11:40 a.m. when Pamela knocked on the door of Big Ron

Triplett's suite. A young secretary answered the door. She was beautiful, blonde and classically shaped. She acted as Triplett's escort whenever he traveled or needed a date for a business occasion. She was definitely a showpiece. Pamela didn't have to guess what other services she provided. The two women surreptitiously studied each other. Each immediately disliking the other and barely concealing it.

Triplett's bodyguards were standing behind the secretary and were quick to step closer as Pamela strolled past her apparent competition. Pamela learned later that the guards had been placed on red alert for the day. One of the members of Triplett's upper echelon was found dead in his bed. Until they knew why, red alert was on.

The two guards asked Pamela to turn around and hold out her arms. They took great pleasure in slowly frisking her. She knew better than to question them, so she just endured. She wondered what Triplett would have to say to the guards had he been aware of their "technique" as they rubbed high along her pants legs. She was wearing tight black pants, stiletto heels and a very revealing white shirt. She looked exceptionally alluring. Pamela could see the pretty young secretary smiling as the men performed their "duty." The search didn't last long but it was still humiliating.

The secretary smiled demurely at Pamela, "The guards are very thorough, aren't they?" Without waiting she pivoted around saying, "This way." Entering his office Triplett was conversing with one of his lieutenants, a stereotypical accountant-type with thick glasses and a deep furrowed brow. The only thing missing was the plastic green visor and a pocket protector. The two men were deeply engaged in a serious conversation.

"Look, it's all black and white. We aren't making our numbers in the elder care business anymore." Triplett had a sharp tone to his voice.

"Yes sir, I know, but..."

"But nothing!" Triplett saw Pamela in the background and motioned for his secretary to take her to his bedroom. Their voices still carried across the suite and Pamela could hear every word.

"Sir, a number of the elder care organizations are heading into Chapter 11 as we speak. There simply isn't the money to be had anymore. Cost is going up and Medicaid isn't paying like the old days. They're cash strapped, too."

"Listen," Triplett was losing his patience. "Start filing more reports to Medicaid. Tell them our patients are receiving physical therapy seven days a week if you have to."

"Mr. Triplett..."

"Hell, for that matter tell them our patients all have arthritis, too. Tell the government we have to give out Jorestat -2 by the handful. Triplett pointed his finger at his lieutenant. "I want numbers, not excuses, you got it?"

"Yes, sir."

"Now get out."

As soon as the door to his suite was shut, Triplett stood up leisurely and stretched. He turned towards his secretary, smiled warmly, and ordered his usual Jack Daniel's and Diet Coke. When she returned he cradled the cold glass in his hand, he savored a few sips and sauntered in to Pamela. She was sitting on the end of bed with her legs crossed and arms folded. She rocked her foot impatiently.

"So, why so formal?" Triplett planted himself directly in front of her. His waist was at her eye level. He stepped closer. "It's been awhile since we've had a chance to relive our Mississippi adventure."

Pamela's eyes slowly drifted up to meet his.

She slowly placed her hand on his hand. "Has it been painful to be without me?"

"Damn straight it has."

"Who's the blonde?" Pamela arched her left brow. "I bet she helped you keep it from being too hard of a time."

"Ok, that's enough whining," Triplett's voice now sounded like when he'd been dealing with his lieutenant. "We've got an hour or two to fool around, eat and talk."

Pamela didn't like to be in a hurry. She was like a crock-pot warming up to the idea. But she knew that Triplett was eager, ready and didn't play games. He was more like an oven that was always set on broil.

It didn't take too long for the crock-pot to change gears. Pamela stood up and stretched her hands across Triplett's chest. Calmly, she unbuttoned his shirt. She planned to make him long for another round like their Mississippi tryst. Soon the headboard was bouncing lightly against the wall. She knew that his desire was soon translated into pleasure. Occasionally, she would purposefully moan loudly knowing that the secretary was probably listening. She did her best to coax her partner into cries of ecstasy and smiled triumphantly when she was rewarded.

Thirty minutes later, Triplett and Pamela were relaxed and satisfied.

After dressing slowly, Pamela walked lazily into the next room and faced the secretary with a look of "freshly satisfied" sex in her eyes. Good sex.

The secretary looked at her watch. "Oh, I see you're ahead of schedule now, Mr. Triplett." She smiled cattily at her boss as she spoke. "Should I order up lunch?"

Pamela was quick to intercede, "We already have plans to eat at the Buckhead Diner."

The secretary pursed her lips, holding back from telling Pamela off.

"I'm afraid that's not possible." Triplett announced.

Pamela glared quickly at him.

"No, today's a bad day for me to be out in public."

"I thought…" Pamela touched his arm.

"Until we find out what or who was behind the death of one of our officers in the Association, it wouldn't be wise for me to be out and about."

Pamela understood and sure didn't want to be in the line of fire.

The secretary spoke up softly. "Perhaps, I should call down to the restaurant and have them prepare her a quick takeout?"

Pamela smiled. "I don't think so, dear." She stepped closer to the secretary. "Why don't you run fetch us a meal from the Italian restaurant down in the lobby. And, do make it quick."

Triplett liked to watch the two women work hard to position themselves in his hierarchy. A true pecking order. He was indeed enjoying this moment.

"I don't think so." The secretary stated back harshly.

"Now ladies," Triplett knew that both of the women had drawn the line. Neither would gracefully back down. He would have to be the one to cast the final vote. He was the one that would make one woman happy and the other one feel cheap.

The women waited for his answer. But, before he could speak, someone knocked on the door.

Immediately the guards moved into action. One guard walked Triplett over to the bedroom, stood in front of him, aiming his gun at the door. The other guard nodded for the secretary to open the door. He stood behind her with his coat open. He had a .38 holstered on his left side.

Another business lieutenant. This one was there to talk about their military fleecing racket. The numbers were down.

Triplett didn't have time for lunch now.

Pamela could leave with her pride intact.

WASHINGTON, D.C.
MAY 2001

"Neil Henry!" The senator stood up, walked out of his office, calling for Neil to follow. "Neil! For God's sake you're slower than molasses in winter."

Neil had been reviewing a bill that was about to come up for a vote in the Senate. It proposed drilling for oil in Alaskan National Forest territory. He knew why the senator wanted him to spend his time on it. The senator would support anything that would help his campaign war chest. Since the oil industry had always supported the senator and they wanted to drill in Alaska, well, the senator wanted them happy. Very happy.

As soon as they were in the limo and the senator's bodyguard/driver closed the door, Neil smirked. "You gotta read some of that Alaskan bill. You'll like it."

The senator asked his driver to take them to the Four Season's restaurant. For a few minutes the senator just looked out his window and watched the clamor of the city. It was in full motion at noontime. People packed the crosswalks and scooted across the streets, dodging cars and taxis. Everyone walked briskly, cell phones glued to their ears.

The senator turned slowly away from his tinted window. "What were you saying about the bill?"

Neil shook his head. "We keep depending on foreign countries for our oil and we are sitting on some of the biggest reserves in the world. We got to drill in Alaska."

"You know as well as I do that when people start getting their power cut off, they'll start screaming at us to drill. In fact, when the gas lines get longer, they'll absolutely demand that we drill." Catfish shook his head. "People don't care about what they can't see. They just don't want to be inconvenienced."

The senator slouched in the black leather seat. His dark blue suit blending with the interior. If by chance they entered a tunnel the senator might visually disappear, except, of course, for his big head and flabby chin. "This may be a good bargaining chip."

Neil pulled on the cuff of his tailor-made suit. "You must support it, but I wouldn't be too loud about it."

"You know how the President views this bill?"

Neil replied. "He said he'd veto it if it passes, but he keeps a low profile on the subject."

"You see, this is a no-brainer piece of legislation from my point of view." The senator paused to emphasize his point. "The President should sign it and get on with things. It's not like we've developed alternative sources of energy. At least not enough to keep our country rolling."

"Of course, health care reform is where he has been high profile."

"Yes," the senator noted, "but how many low profiles do we have to deliver to change his mind on one high profile? We have to find a number of bills that he favors and we don't give two bits about and see if we can help him pass them."

Neil pulled on his coat cuff again and then picked off a little piece of lint on his pants. "You think he'll bend? He seems determined to change the health care system."

"I don't know. I doubt it, but if he does the White House has an army of public relations people. They'll find him a back door. They'll spin it to make him look like a hero if he shifts course."

"How could you stand to make Hillgren a hero?"

"Be that as it may," The senator straightened as the limo approached the Four Seasons. "We have one priority… he has many."

The limo driver ran quickly around to open the door. A few reporters were hanging around the front of the hotel ready to blast a few questions.

Neil stopped the senator from getting out too quickly so that they could finish their conversation on this topic. "So you want me to figure out which bills we can pull together to make an offer that Hillgren can't refuse?"

"No. I want you to figure out which of them Vice President Lancaster can't refuse." The senator continued speaking as he got out of the car. "Remember, if Hillgren won't bend, a divided presidential team will create chaos."

Neil knew that creating chaos was simply another form of stalling.

The senator held up his index finger. Neil noticed how stained his fingertips were. They were a brownish-yellow from decades of cigars. "Vice President Lancaster is a liberal at heart. Offer him enough of that socialistic crap and he'll take the bait. We just have to make sure it's the pork belly stuff that we are selling. We can't give in on a major deal. At least, not unless it's our last draw."

The senator didn't answer any shouted questions by the reporters. He was on his way to a very important meeting. Walking briskly into the restaurant with Neil running to catch up, they were seated immediately.

"I've asked somebody to join us." The senator was looking around to see if his guest had arrived. He waived for the waiter.

The distinguished looking waiter had a slight French accent. The waiter showed them to a table near some windows but the senator refused. Instead the senator asked for a darker corner table."

By the time they were seated and settled, the expected guest was escorted to their table.

Neil recognized the face but didn't recall the name. The man was African-American with a neatly trimmed mustache and a clean-shaven head. A good-looking tall man wearing a well-fitted Armani suit. His tie had to cost over two hundred dollars. His gold and diamond Rolex was barely peeking out from the edge of his French-cuffed shirt.

"Hello, Senator."

His deeply resonating voice sounded like a TV anchorman or a jazz station disk jockey. His voice was smooth without identifiable accent.

Neil stood up and shook his hand. "I'm Neil Henry."

The man returned the handshake. "Call me Larry." He didn't add his last name nor did he feel compelled to give it. He sat down keeping his back to the wall. It was his nature to be cautious.

Larry straightened his silverware. He didn't bother to put his napkin in his lap. "Listen, I'm short on time so if you don't mind gentlemen, I'd like to get down to business."

The senator liked to go at his own pace. He waited until after the waiter took their order. Larry passed on the food. The senator got a rib eye steak, rare, and a baked potato. Neil wanted something on the light side and ended up ordering salmon.

"Larry," the senator said casually as if accustomed to talking with Colburn many times in the past, "I'm thinking that we have an opportunity to have a win-win situation."

Larry waited expectantly.

Perhaps it was the way the man looked at the senator, or perhaps it was his voice that Neil finally recognized. "You're Larry Colburn."

Colburn looked at Neil like it was about time he figured it out. Colburn was a high profile lawyer and was well known across the nation. He had been on talk shows and the news for years. The only reason Neil hadn't recognized him sooner was that he had changed his appearance. Colburn only recently shaved his head and grew a mustache.

Colburn was irritated that Neil recognized him. Not that he was trying to hide from the public, it was quiet the opposite. He was a media hound. But he had been in the media too much. He needed a new look. His old look had saturated the market. His public relations person wanted the change. It was their idea to stir up the photographers on Colburn's new style. It would make all the entertainment magazines by the end of the week. Besides, if he were trying to hide from the media, he certainly wouldn't have met with Senator Adams at a public restaurant.

Colburn was known for winning employment discrimination suits against large companies. His record was perfect. It started with a multi-million dollar verdict for one employee against a manufacturing company. Next he was the mastermind behind a class-action lawsuit that led to a 200 million dollar settlement. The charges were racial discrimination. He won the case in Mississippi with a mostly white jury. Later, he won a case during an election year against a newspaper company that Charles Henderson owned. Henderson was Senator Adams opponent that year.

"What is your idea, Senator?" Colburn asked.

"Well, according to the statistics, I see that workers who bring employment lawsuits are increasingly victorious."

"And where do you want me to investigate?"

"I want you to look hard at Greystone Medical School and Hospital."

"And if I don't find anything?"

"Look harder." The senator emphasized quickly.

Colburn returned the verbal volley. "And, if I still don't find anything?"

The senator put his silverware aside. "Well then, I guess you'll need to be resourceful, won't you?"

Colburn nodded. "Just like old times, right Senator?"

The senator didn't reply. He was waiting for Colburn to bring up the bottom line issue. Money. Just how badly did the senator need Colburn's services this time?

"So, Senator, I assume that if I accept this job, we'll have the standard agreement."

The senator nodded. The senator would provide a non-refundable retainer of one million dollars, win or lose. In addition, if Colburn made the case and won an award, he could kept it all.

CHAPTER 9

CHARLOTTE, NORTH CAROLINA
MAY 2001

NEW YORK City was ages ago. After the homeless man ran from the abandoned building with a small CD case stuffed under his coat, he checked periodically to make sure the disks were safe and sound. They were. The disks were his lotto tickets. He just knew it. A big time, fat lotto prize for sure. They had to be worth a lot for someone to get killed over them. All he had to do was deliver them to this guy, Barringer. It took a long time to thumb his way to Charlotte.

A light misty, drizzle was in the air. The day was gray and now as the darkness took hold the homeless man worked the street for a few coins. East Boulevard saw few homeless. The rich and poor were but a few miles apart. The famous Dilworth area of Charlotte was juxtaposed to the poorer areas.

"Got a few coins to spare?" The homeless man stood outside a liquor store and asked a teenager dressed like he just bought out Abercrombie. "I just need a cup of coffee."

"Sure." The teen replied as he studied the homeless man. He had long red dreadlocks and wore army fatigues. "Come over here, Dread-Mon." The young man nicknamed him.

They walked to the side of the store, pausing near the dumpsters. "Listen, Dread-Mon, let's make a deal. I need you to buy me some beer."

"And if I do?"

"I'll pay you."

"How much?"

"Twenty."

Dread-Mon smiled. "How much beer ya want?"

The teen looked around before answering. "I'm having a party and we need a case of beer and a half gallon of Vodka."

"No problem." Dread-Mon stuck out his dirty hand.

"I'm gonna give you sixty bucks and you better bring me back the booze and the change."

"Sure."

The homeless man watched as the three crisp twenty dollar bills were placed in his hand. He wanted to smell them, as if they were ripe tomatoes. "It'll only take a few minutes."

The teen nodded. "I'll be watching."

"Yeah, sure." Dread-Mon turned and vanished into the liquor store.

The money was burning a hole in his pocket. He looked around at the different liquors. He grabbed a case of beer and a half gallon of cheap Vodka. Dread-Mon pocketed a pint of whiskey and some of the change.

He paid for the booze and returned to the dumpster. He was looking forward to completing his deal with the kid. Dread-Mon thought about the taste of the whiskey, a warm meal and some cash to get a bus ticket down to Atlanta. His lotto was waiting.

The teen was pacing back and forth, clearly agitated. Three steps right, three steps left. Back and forth.

"Did ya get the goods?" The teen shouted.

Dread-Mon was bewildered. They were only a few feet from each other and the kid was shouting. Then it dawned on him. It was like slow motion movie. Another man who was crouched by the dumpster stood up and placed his hand on the pistol at his side. A cop.

"Put the package down and get down on the ground." The cop directed.

Dread-Mom should have known better. "Whoa man... don't get carried away. I'll do it."

Dread-Mom had that "been there and done that" syndrome written all over his face. He did exactly what the cop asked and made sure that everyone could see his hands at all times. No fast moves.

The teen was a damn set-up.

Less than an hour later Dread-Mon got processed for a jail cell. He would get to visit until trial time unless he could make bail. And the chances of that happening were slim to none. Of course, the cops found the CD case. There was a note on the inside of the case addressed to Dr. William Barringer at Greystone University Hospital in Atlanta, Georgia. One of the undercover officers was assigned to follow-up and see if the CD's had been stolen from Barringer or just lost.

The officer assigned to the case had plenty to do without having to track down some doctor in Atlanta over a few CD's. Ridiculous. If it were truly important the doctor in Atlanta would have a backup system. It was beyond annoying to think the sargent wanted him to use up his valuable time on a follow-up of some burned out homeless guy. Simple solution. For the time being he put the CD case into a drawer and moved on to more pressing matters, like the rape and murder case he's been hot on lately. He figured he would let a little time pass and then just mail the stupid thing.

CHAPTER 10

LAWRENCEVILLE, GEORGIA
MAY 2001

JAKE WAS great to have around the ranch. He looked forward everyday to visiting and playing with John. Often he would watch John while Connie and Bill rode their horses. While he would watch John he would sit for hours with a ballgame on and thumb through the thousands of players cards he had collected, organizing them according to team, year, position and alphabet. His rookie Mickey Mantle card was his claim to fame. The special cards were framed and hung smartly throughout his room adjacent to the barn. He made sure Connie knew about them so after he was long gone and John had grown up she could pass them on to him.

Jake took his time explaining each player to the future lad of baseball. It didn't matter if the boy never understood, Jake would pretend like John was listening to every word. He told stories of how he used to go to the minor league games on weekends. Picture perfect days. Those games were a thrill and he could give a play by play of a great game as if it was happening right now. Jake was in the midst of one of his stories as Bill and Connie slipped out of the house to go riding.

At the stable, Bill gave Connie a little kiss on the neck and a hug.

Her response was half hearted. It was the type of response that let Bill know he had to explore deeper. Not right away, he knew that he couldn't hurry her. She hated to be pressured into telling how she felt. All in good time.

Bill and Connie had their own hobby. They both loved to ride. Bill's favorite horse was an Arabian named Bojangles. He was a beautiful white with obvious pride and strength. Connie owned a black, shiny, thoroughbred mare named Stina. A clever horse with dark, mysterious brown eyes. Any horse enthusiast would admire her slender and graceful lines.

They were walking the horses out the back gate when Connie broke their unwritten rule of bringing up serious topics while riding. The purpose of riding was to get away from the day-to-day stress and demands of this world. "I have something I want to talk about."

Bill was surprised that Connie was already starting to open up. He figured that it would be night before she started telling him what was on her mind.

"I got some bad news yesterday," she revealed.

They mounted their horses as she continued. "As soon as I showed up at John's daycare, the director asked to see me."

Bill's heart sank. The director had been concerned that John's condition was worsening. This was the best daycare they could find for John. Bill didn't know of a better place.

Bill pulled back on Bojangles' spirited desire to run through the pasture and down the main stretch of an old dirt road that circled Bill's property. The road circled their one hundred plus acres of land. Bojangles always ran certain stretches and this was his favorite.

Connie waited until Bojangles settled down. "Well, I hate to say it but John was expelled."

"What?" Bill's worst fears were confirmed.

"They said that he continues to bite other kids. They can't stop him."

"You got to be kidding me!" Bill was angry. "We pay them a small fortune and they have the gall to dismiss him for biting?" With an anger taking hold Bill decided it was time for a ride. "Let's go I need to move."

They let the horses run longer than usual, until Bill finally stopped. Connie pulled up beside him. Both horses were breathing hard in the cool air, twisting their heads and slinging foam from their mouths.

"Ok, I feel better now. So what else is eating you, honey?"

"Well," Connie let her feet dangle out of her stirrups to stretch her legs. "I don't think I enjoy..."

Bill had learned to wait for Connie to spit it out.

Connie took a deep breath. "I really don't think I enjoy medicine anymore." Her eyes teared with frustration. "I feel like I'm going through the motions. My heart isn't in it anymore."

"Do you know why?"

"Not really." Connie shook her head. "At least it's nothing that I can say for sure. I mean, sure we can all point to the obvious." Connie took a short glance at Bill. "It's easy to blame the system. I hate the paperwork. I hate the revolving door for patients instead of developing relationships and caring for them for the long term. One minute you have a patient and then the next minute they're switched to a different managed care system and zap they're gone. I hate having some administrator second-guessing my medical decisions based on cost instead of need. I hate the term "market-forces" that I hear all the time."

Connie inhaled deeply again "Somewhere along the line it just quit being fun. I actually dread going to the office."

Bill listened patiently, not commenting.

Connie held Stina at a complete stop. "Bill, I know what you're thinking. You think that I'm just tired and that by the end of the weekend I'll be recharged. You think that you've seen these mood swings before and that this too will be swept underneath the rug."

Bill didn't want to be cornered on this one, but she could always read his mind. "Something like that."

Connie turned Stina around and signaled her to walk back to the barn. Bill and Bojangels followed.

"Well, it's not the same this time. I really am making a change in my life."

Connie sounded determined. "I want to be more involved with John. Especially now, I want to be there for him. No more daycare. And we both know that he's going to need a lot of help to learn the basics."

Bill followed, "You want to stay at home?"

Connie nodded. Her eyes looked determined. "You know that once I make up my mind I go forward. To tell you the truth, I think I would find something else to do even if John was fine."

"When do you plan on turning in your resignation?" Bill asked softly.

Connie smiled. "I turned it in yesterday afternoon."

Bill's mouth dropped open. He shook his head as if he was trying to absorb what she said. "You resigned?"

"Yes, Bill, I did."

The rest of the ride was silent.

Just the muffled sound of horse hooves on the dirt.

———◆———

It was almost eleven in the evening and Bill looked around for Connie. She was in the study, a glass of wine was next to the computer. Deep in thought, she stared at the computer screen.

"I'm heading to bed." Bill said.

Connie turned to see Bill in the doorway. "I'll be with you in a minute. I want to finish this letter."

"You're writing a letter?"

"I thought I would write and tell Vance of my decision."

Bill nodded that he thought it was a good idea.

Bill watched as Connie began to type. He backed away quietly and went to bed.

Connie finished her letter but when she read it, the words sounded clumsy and impersonal. It read like a technical article. She crumbled the letter and tossed it into the trash can. She knew what she had written didn't capture what she really wanted to say. She turned off her computer without saving anything. Searching her desk she found a pen and some rice paper that she occasionally used to write family and friends. She left the study and sat at the kitchen table. This time her words flowed. This time there were no long pauses between sentences. Her letter was short and reflective.

Dear Vance,

You have been my mentor and friend for many years and I have always counted on you for counsel on important decisions, but I had to do what I describe in this letter myself.

I have decided to leave my practice. I know you're shocked at this but you can probably guess my reasons:

For years you have been speaking about the medical, legal, industrial, political complex. This complex as it is today has changed our medical field into a business instead of a professional service. I am no longer allowed to care for patients the way you taught me to do. Vance, I can no longer tolerate this.

Second, I cannot leave John at the daycare center another day. It is clear to me that a mother's love and tenderness cannot be packaged and duplicated by even the most dedicated daycare experts. He needs me and I need him.

Vance, you and Jennifer mean everything to me. I still have a warm feeling every time I look at the plaque with the leaf you gave me from the island of Kos. Giving me a leaf, from the very tree under which Hippocrates stood and taught, will forever act as a reminder of the pursuit for excellence. Some how I believe that Hippocrates himself would understand my problem and my resolution. I hope and believe you will understand.

Much Love—Connie

WASHINGTON, D.C.
MAY 2001

A commercial flight on Saturday evening should have been empty, but with two previous flights cancelled due to mechanical problems, the jet was packed. Neil Henry had decided to go see Pamela. It was his weekend and even though she was staying in Atlanta for a few weeks, a deal was a deal. She agreed to let him come down and stay with her for the evening.

It had been a long time since Neil had flown with a commercial airline. He was particularly upset when the flight couldn't accommodate a first class seat. At least he had an aisle seat.

Neil felt confined. He could barely tolerate the couple of hours it would take to get to Atlanta. He managed to take it in stride when the captain announced that there would be a few minutes delay on their departure to allow a restocking of the flight attendant station. But forty-five minutes later Neil was outraged that the jet still was at the gate. The captain finally announced that there was a defective light on his control panel and they were waiting on a maintenance crew. The captain estimated another thirty minutes or so.

The cabin was hot and the air was stagnant. Neil took off his tie and coat, but he still felt sweaty. He was in no mood to listen to the child next to him while she hummed non-stop nursery songs and chewed her gum like a hungry camel. He sure didn't enjoy hearing her hefty father snoring peacefully like a sumo wrestler. Finally the jet made it onto the runway. Neil almost cheered when the flight took off. To add insult to injury the flight attendant handed him a little bag of pretzels and a glass of soda. Neil was hungry and the pretzels didn't help.

Eighty miles outside of Atlanta they were put in a holding pattern for thirty minutes. Then, to top it off, when they finally did land they had to sit on the tarmac because another jet had parked at their gate. By the time Neil made it to the Grand Hyatt in Buckhead, it was nearly nine o'clock.

Pamela looked at her watch, "If we hurry we can make our dinner reservation."

"Hey!" Neil almost thought he had the wrong lady. "You're blonde!"

Pamela nodded. "Had it done this afternoon." She turned to model her new style.

Neil admired her hair for a few minutes and then hurriedly moved his luggage out of the foyer and into the bedroom while Pamela poured him a stiff gin and tonic.

They were in the elevator going down as Neil noticed how beautiful Pamela looked tonight. She looked different. More vibrant than usual. Probably because of her hair.

"You… you really are stunning." Neil studied her more closely. She had her hair up. It looked sophisticated. "I do love the look."

"That's good because now I'm one hundred percent blonde, Neil."

Neil dropped his jaw. "You mean that you…"

Pamela winked suggestively. "That's right. I matched the collar with the cuffs."

The elevator door slid open snapping Neil back to reality. Moving out of the elevator, Neil looked at her dress. It was white with wide black stripes. It had a classy Spanish look. Breezy and flowing.

Pamela had already lined up a limo for the night.

She wanted to eat dinner and go dancing.

Before Neil could finish his drink and get comfortable, the driver pulled up in front of the building that housed the restaurant. After a short elevator ride down to the basement the doors opened into a bombardment of the wonderful rich smells of authentic Italian cuisine, all the wonders of garlic, exotic spices and the finest fresh herbs made a tantalizing blend. The patrons were in high spirits, toasting each other with fine Italian wines. After they were escorted to their table, Neil ordered a bottle of Rothschild '85.

Neil was still getting use to Pamela's new look. She would not have changed her hair if it had not been for a damned good cause. She was on the hunt and she wanted to bag a real trophy. Neil knew she was ambitious but not even he thought she could have scored a serious operator like Triplett. But, then again, she hadn't actually scored him yet.

Half way into the Rothschild, Pamela tried to get the scoop on Senator Adams.

"Is everything going according to plan?" Pamela asked.

"Yes." Neil knew that Pamela was doing what he had taught her so well to do. Obtain information. Information was power and protection.

"I met with Vice President Lancaster again and he assured me that he could get you on with Connelly's team as the head of CIS."

"Has the President met with Connelly yet?"

"No, according to the Vice President they have a meeting scheduled next week."

Pamela asked the waiter to bring another bottle of wine as their food arrived.

They ate their Caesar salad slowly and then took their time with the main course, a combination for two with small portions of salmon fettuccine, grilled sea bass and rack of lamb.

Pamela was able to squeeze Neil for the information about the senator's plan with Larry Colburn. She was always impressed with the manipulative mind of the honorable Senator Adams. A true genius. A true Catfish.

By the time they finished their meal Neil was already three sheets in the wind. His words slurred. The combination of travel, gin and wine took its toll. Pamela ordered him an after dinner drink. A white Russian. She ordered one for herself to keep her nerves steady.

WASHINGTON, D.C.
MAY 2001

Vance felt the power and influence of the presidency every time he walked into the White House. A palpable aura of tradition and energy. He felt younger and stronger. Bill and Quincy were invited to come to visit as well. The three of them were to talk with the President over dinner and then have dessert on the Truman balcony.

Walking back to the Oval Office, they were joined by the Vice President. The next topic of conversation was about the subcommittee that Vance would head. The president stood tall in front of Vance. Some people have an air about them, an assured presence that naturally projects confidence and power. Vance noticed that the President had grown in this manner. The President's presence could be felt from across the room. You wanted to approach the president and bask in the power he so majestically exuded.

Once everyone was introduced, each found a place in the sitting area. The president sat in a rocker just as John Kennedy did. Bill and Quincy found a sofa together. The Vice President and Vance took to the chairs.

The President started the conversation. "Recently, I received a call from Senator Adams. His call was inspired by a small coalition of senators trying to derail our efforts, Vance."

"That doesn't surprise me, Mr. President."

"I didn't think it would." President Hillgren picked up a folder marked Subcommittee for Health Reform, Chairman: Dr. Vance Connelly. "In short, Adams is pushing for so-called fiscal responsibility. He said that the present system isn't broken, the industry just needs more competition."

"And what do you think, Mr. President?" Quincy spoke up boldly.

"I don't know. That's why I've asked for your subcommittee to explore what we need to do to fix our problems."

"Adams is right." Bill inserted, "Whatever we suggest will probably cost a huge amount."

The Vice President was jotting down notes. He was average-sized with classic Swedish cheekbones, grey hair and blue eyes. At the moment he seemed to avoid eye contact with Vance even when he spoke directly to him. "The president doesn't want you to be financially constrained. He wants solutions. Real solutions. Leave it to the financial subcommittee to figure out the source of money. The president wants to develop the best health care system in the world."

The President agreed. "Precisely. I want a vision of the health care future at its best. Leave it to me to sell the vision to the American people."

CHAPTER 11

ATLANTA, GEORGIA
OCTOBER 1952

BY 4:00 a.m. Vance was up and pouring his first cup of coffee. He always liked it black and strong. The old percolator was slow but the hot, fresh flavor and the familiar aroma was worth the wait. Almost without effort Vance would wake up five minutes before the alarm clock was set to go off and roll gently out of the bed and head toward the coffee.

Vance never found it difficult getting up early or getting by with four to five hours of sleep. In fact, he figured any person with heartfelt purpose was pulled, like a magnet, to their work. And he always had plenty of work and a full tank of inspiration to match.

Vance liked structure and he learned to associate different rooms of his home with different aspects of his work. The den, which held his favorite large leather chair, was for reading his medical journals and writing. The den was cozy with wood paneling and a large fireplace which made it warm and comfortable. The living room was just for thinking. He always took his first cup of coffee in the morning in the living room and sat in his designated thinking chair.

The living room was large and adjoined the dining room, which made the room appear even larger. The focal point for his thinking room was a fireplace and mantle. He particularly liked the paintings he had collected during his travels. His favorite painting was a Van Gogh reproduction. The splash of colors captured the feelings of spring, youth, and new beginnings.

The lights remained off when he sat in his thinking chair. He felt the darkness and the stillness of the early morning and, initially, he would just let his thoughts roll around without structure. Soon something would surface. And then, it would happen. Like a master of chess, Vance would visualize a continuous stream of potential options. He could see an event unfold as if it was actually happening right then. Fifteen or twenty chess moves in advance. Conversations. People's faces. A new diagnosis or treatment for a patient or a different sentence for the scientific article he was writing.

This morning there was a full moon. Vance always left the curtains open, allowing the shadows of tree limbs to march through the window and cast abstract designs on the floor. He contemplated the complexity of the patterns, realizing that his thoughts were not free-floating. They were focused on the Robert Lancaster case. The pieces somehow didn't seem to fit. Yet, like a writer's block, Vance was unable to place his finger on what exactly disturbed him so deeply.

Cameron set his alarm clock to get an early start. Even with the shrill reminder he usually turned over and faded back to sleep. There were no structured routines for Cameron. When he was given a case he was free to adjust his lifestyle to do whatever was necessary to enforce the law. His only requirement was to call into the office whenever possible and give an update on his progress. Often his cases were politically delicate. He was known for busting wealthy businessmen with money-laundering schemes. He had made his share of stings on high profile figures who took major government kickbacks.

At seven o'clock in the morning Cameron sat up in the bed and reached for a pack of cigarettes. He always liked that first Camel of the morning. Deeply inhaling, the smoke cleared the last remnants of sleep and he began to plan his day.

He picked up the phone and dialed a number that he knew by heart. As soon as his party answered, Cameron started talking. He didn't bother with a "hello" or "good morning", just jumped right into his conversation. "Listen, Big Eddie, I want some information and I need it now."

Big Eddie sighed and cleared his throat, "What the hell are you doing calling me at this ungodly time in the morning? This better be important. What kind of information do you want?"

"The kind that you can help me with."

There was no reply.

"Hey, all I'm asking is to meet with you." Cameron eased his cigarette ashes into a half-empty beer bottle left from the night before. "I'll owe you one."

Big Eddie wasn't much for conversations, especially when he was hung over and tired. His voice deepened. "You'll owe me more than one. What is it this time?"

"A man by the name of Robert Lancaster may have been helped out of a six story window Sunday night."

"Yeah, I remember reading about that in the newspaper. The story is that he jumped."

"What do you think the administrators at Greystone wanted them to say? Anyway before I declare it a suicide, I just want to make sure that Lancaster wasn't connected with the wrong kind of business."

"So, what makes you think that this guy—"

"Robert Lancaster."

"Right, Robert Lancaster." Big Eddie almost sounded curious. "Why would you think that a man like that would have anything to do with the wrong side of the street?"

"A man like what?"

"You know, the paper said he was a big businessman type."

Cameron dropped his cigarette into the bottle, lighting another one before the smoke from the first one cleared. "I figure that there are only two possibilities in this case, Big Eddie. Either he committed suicide or…"

"Or he was helped?" Big Eddie finished Cameron's sentence for him.

"Right, and if he wasn't connected to the wrong side of the tracks, well then—-" Cameron rolled out of bed, gave himself a good scratch and stretched. He was wearing a pair of blue boxers and white socks. His back and shoulders were laced with thick muscles. "Then, I believe this case might get real interesting."

Vance had told his secretary that he didn't want to be disturbed. That didn't last long. She let him know that Lieutenant Lee was on the phone.

Vance put down his pen and leaned back in his chair and took the call.

As soon as Vance said hello, Cameron got down to business. "I have a couple of questions." There was no beating around the bush with this man.

Before Cameron could give his first question, Vance interrupted. "I got some news first. I've been interviewing the nurses and I've found out that several visitors had been seen around the time of the crime."

Cameron stopped in his tracks. "Go on."

"Unfortunately the nurses didn't get a good look at them but they know that one was an Oriental woman and the other one was a tall man."

Cameron hated descriptions that were so vague. How many people in the world would that fit? God why can't people be more observant. At least he knows there were some people lingering around.

"Do you know where Jennifer Eden is?" Cameron asked.

Vance checked his watch. "She works the night shift."

"I know, but she didn't show up for work last night." Cameron wanted to show that he had done his homework. "Her personnel file indicates that she never misses work."

"She's not at home?"

"If she is, she won't answer the phone." Cameron drilled down further. "Did she know Robert Lancaster personally?"

"No, at least I don't think so."

Cameron recalled the conversation that he had with the old nurse on the elevator. "Tell me, doctor, do nurses typically call a patient by their first name?"

"No, almost never. Why?"

"Just wondering. I'll drive out to Miss Eden's place later." Cameron jumped to another topic. He asked Vance to go over the medical details one more time with Wasserman. Cameron knew he wouldn't understand most of them anyway.

After Vance hung up he asked his secretary to see if Dr. Wassermann could stop by sometime after lunch. He also asked her to get Jennifer Eden on the phone.

His secretary was unable to get in touch with Jennifer, but said she would call every thirty minutes throughout the day. She also missed Wassermann by about fifteen minutes. Wednesday was his golf day. Although the ground was still wet from the rains earlier in the week, the skies were clear and the temperature stayed around 58°. It was perfect for a dedicated golfer like Wassermann.

Vance asked his secretary to leave a message at Wasserman's club. He would arrive at the club's card room around 5:30 p.m. Vance figured that Wassermann would get the message at the ninth hole and would call if the plan was inconvenient.

Cameron dug his hands deep into his pockets as he approached the table of Big Eddie Zimbardo. Big Eddie was the owner of Zimbardo's, a nice club in midtown Atlanta. He was always nice to the cops because he wanted protection for his business establishments. Zimbardo's was a great meeting place and business was booming. He catered to the upward, mobile type of executive. By noon everyday the place was packed. Three-martini lunches were the order of the day. Big Eddie loved his club, but he loved his private-eye agency more. That was his first line of business and he never gave it up. He was a hustler since childhood and being in the private-eye business had advantages. Big Eddie had something on every major political figure in Atlanta.

He was a weight lifter, weighing in at about 280 pounds of mostly muscle. His thinning hair was slicked down and jet-black. A bullfrog voice seemed appropriate coming from his short, thick neck. Big Eddie ate a sandwich and potato chips while watching a shapely college-aged girl sing his favorite song. Big Eddie was known for his top of the line entertainment talent. He was also known for peddling prostitution on the side.

Cameron stood about three feet away. "If you keep eating like that you'll get fat." He watched with amusement as the man peered up from his plate, mayonnaise still clinging to the corners of his mouth.

Big Eddie choked down a bite of sandwich. "Don't worry. I work it off." He wiped his mouth with the back of his hand.

Cameron sat next to him and glanced up at the young woman standing next to a piano player. She was singing an upbeat song, slightly out of tune but looking sexy.

"What do you think Lieutenant? Is she a pretty gal, or what?"

Cameron's eyes trailed the woman's figure from her uplifted breasts to the curve at the small of her back. He admired the firm roundness below it.

Before Cameron answered Big Eddie gave a short belly laugh. "Damn right she's a beautiful babe."

Big Eddie took another vicious bite out of his sandwich and talked while he was chewing. "Believe it or not, Cameron, that gal is studying to be an accountant."

Cameron couldn't help but watch her as she sang. Her hips swayed to the music.

"Fortunately for me," Big Eddie wiped his plate clean with his finger, "she needed some fast money. Of course when she found out what she could make dancin' and singin', well she's no dummy."

"She'll probably never finish school either." Cameron had heard that story one too many times.

Big Eddie laughed hard again.

Cameron looked over at a young woman who reminded him of an old girlfriend. She was serving sandwiches and beer at a back bar. He made a mental note to talk with her sometime. He caught her eye and waived for a beer.

"Did you find some information for me?" Cameron asked.

Big Eddie looked hard into Cameron's eyes. "Yeah, I can help ya a little. But, what's in it for Big Eddie?"

"I understand you had a little trouble with some prostitution charges the other night."

Big Eddie smiled.

Cameron leaned closer. "I can get those girls a clean bill of health."

"Well, I like being able to take care of my girls. It builds loyalty." Big Eddie rubbed his broad chin. "Ok, it's a deal."

The waitress Cameron had flagged walked up and handed him a cold Budweiser. Big Eddie offered her his dirty dishes and waited until she left.

"So, here's all I know." Big Eddie took a hard gulp of beer. "Apparently your man Robert Lancaster had overextended himself."

"In what way?"

"Word has it that he had the fever."

The back of Cameron's neck was burning again. "So, he liked to gamble, did he?"

"Yep, he had the fever real bad."

"Numbers?"

Big Eddie took another gulp of beer and burped loudly. "Na, he bet on the games. Sports were killing him."

"Was he drowning in debt?"

"That's right," Big Eddie polished off the rest of his beer. "They were about to close him out unless he could come up with $50,000."

"So, instead of having money like I originally thought, he was about to lose it all."

Big Eddie shrugged his shoulders. "He had one option."

"Don't tell me."

"Yep, he borrowed from James Evian."

Cameron sighed heavily. "You know you're desperate when you have to go to the biggest loan shark in Atlanta."

Cameron considered the situation as Big Eddie turned his attention to another girl on stage. So, Robert Lancaster was hedging his bets. Wassermann mentioned that Lancaster was about to land a big banking deal. Maybe Lancaster thought he could pull off the deal and pay off everybody. Cameron wanted to know if Lancaster was the big dreamer type. Always optimistic and always just one day away from selling the big deal or winning the long-shot bet that would make him rich. If the bank deal crashed then maybe Evian collected the hard way.

"I need a meeting with Evian." Cameron pushed away the last half of his beer and stood up.

"And I suppose you want me to set it up?"

"The sooner the better."

"Well, Cameron, when I see that my girls are cleared, you'll get your meeting."

"Your girls will be here by dinner."

"And you'll be meeting Evian tonight."

Cameron nodded, stuffed his hands back into his pockets and headed for the door. He briefly looked for the girl at the back bar and sighed when he couldn't find her.

Vance stopped at the security station at the gate of Wasserman's golf club and identified himself. Apparently Wassermann had received his message and notified the guard. After parking his car he walked by the gardens in front of the mansion-style clubhouse. The clubhouse made the Governor's mansion look small and plain. Vance knew that the golf shop and the locker room were in the back so he walked around the building. Just before the locker room there was a polished mahogany bar showcasing a new Crosley television set with a 10 inch screen. It was surrounded by a half dozen card tables and chairs made from Norwegian yellow wood. Wassermann was sitting with three others reminiscing about their golf outing. He saw Vance at the doorway and flagged him over.

Wassermann had a big smile across his face as he poked out his little chin in victory. Introductions were nothing more than a handshake and then Vance listened to them finish reliving their day.

Vance finally looked at Wassermann. "Listen, Harold, I've got to discuss some business with you."

The others were fast to take the hint and slid over to another table.

Wassermann held up the score card again. "Bet this one will change my handicap a bit."

Vance nodded but decided not to fuel any small talk. "We've got to go over the Robert Lancaster case again."

Wassermann dropped his head for a brief moment. "Again? I told everything I could remember in the presentation."

"Well, there are a few things that I don't understand."

"Like what?" Wassermann sounded irritated.

"Well, you said that you had been his physician for a while."

"When I moved here, I became his physician." Wassermann folded his golf card in half. "I also saw his wife, Victoria, as a patient a few years ago."

"What was wrong with her?"

"She had a few emotional problems. She was a nice person and needed someone to talk to. I'm afraid that she really needs help now. She went to pieces when I told her about her husband."

Vance watched as Wassermann folded his card a second time. "And you don't believe Mr. Lancaster was having angina prior to recently?"

"No." Wassermann finally put his score card into his pocket.

"How do you know that?"

"Actually, Robert Lancaster was a member out here. He played golf every Saturday and Sunday that he was in town." Wassermann looked around the room and nodded to some of the other members. "In fact, I played with him a good bit and he never complained."

Wasserman's weak chin was tucked back toward his neck. He stared downward. "I even tried to teach Victoria how to play golf."

"Why you?"

"Because Robert didn't have the patience. He had a fury of a temper."

"Explosive temper?"

"Yes."

"Enough that he would get physical?"

"I'd say," Wassermann sighed deeply, "I remember one time when we were playing golf and he took a brand new club and slammed it against a tree. He broke the club in half and threw it into the lake."

Vance pulled out a pad and jotted down a few notes. "Is this why you gave him a light sedative at the hospital?"

"Absolutely. I didn't see any signs of depression and I knew that his impatience and temper would flare up because of that big deal he was working on."

For the next forty-five minutes Vance reviewed the case with Wassermann. Everything had been done according to the guidelines. The only new piece of information that surfaced was the fact that Wassermann and Lancaster were apparently friends.

Cameron stopped at a hamburger joint and bought a burger and fries for dinner. His usual. He ate while driving through the bottle-necked traffic on Peachtree. Mustard and ketchup decorated his shirt.

Jennifer Eden's apartment was on the outskirts of Atlanta. When he arrived, the lights were on and he could hear music. Cameron knocked lightly.

He heard someone scrambling to the door. "Who is it?" The

cautious voice was female.

"Lieutenant Lee." Cameron replied loudly.

There was a long pause before Cameron heard the safety lock snap. The door opened a crack. "What do you want?"

"I need to ask you a few questions that all."

"Let me see your badge."

Cameron saw one eye glaring from behind the door.

"Where's the badge?" Her voice was louder and more demanding.

Cameron pulled out his badge and held it up to her eye level. The door opened slowly. A young woman, perhaps in her early twenties, stood in the doorway. She was the same height and had the same hair color as Jennifer's. Even their facial features were similar.

She invited Cameron to step inside. He walked in, quickly scanning the room. It looked like a two-bedroom apartment. Standard furniture. Leather couch. Kitchen table and four chairs. There were feminine frills and knickknacks all around. The stuff that drove Cameron crazy even though everything was neat and in its place.

The young woman marched back to her chair. She was wearing a pair of blue slacks and an untucked, oversized shirt. "I'm her sister, Brooke."

Although Brooke didn't say it, Cameron figured that she was younger than Jennifer by two or three years. They were strikingly similar except that Brooke was a little heavier, more rounded. The phone rang, but Brooke made no move to answer it.

After the fifth ring Cameron looked over at the phone. "Aren't you going to answer it?"

"No, it's been ringing all day and Jennifer told me to leave it alone."

"Where's Jennifer?" Cameron scanned the room again. "And, just when does your sister plan to return?"

"On Sunday."

"Where did she go?"

"I'm not supposed to tell."

Cameron looked sternly. "I'm not just anyone."

"I know, but…"

"Listen Miss…"

Brooke said disdainfully. "Actually I prefer to be called Brooke."

Cameron studied her for a moment. "Listen Brooke, your sister is needed to clear up an investigation."

Brooke folded her arms across her chest with determination. "I know, she told me all about the suicide…"

"Murder."

Brooke froze.

Cameron had not officially declared the case murder, but he knew that saying it would shake up Brooke. "Jennifer is critical to this case."

Brooke needed a minute and excused herself to go to the bathroom.

Cameron nodded and then watched Brooke disappear into the bedroom.

Looking around, Cameron saw a camera next to the telephone. That was like waiving a red flag in front of a bull. It was too irresistible. An exposed roll of film, when developed, could tell a lot about a person. Especially someone who decided to take a fast vacation. He slipped over to the camera and saw two rolls of exposed film. He heard Brooke making her way back into the den. He grabbed the rolls of film and put them in his pocket before returning to his original position.

"Listen, Lieutenant, my sister gave me specific instructions not to disturb her for a few days. That's all she's asking."

"So, you know where she is?"

"No, not exactly." Brooke was careful not to reveal that she knew where Jennifer was. "Well, she calls in to me. I don't know how to call her."

Cameron looked at the phone. "But you just said that you're not answering the phone."

Brooke started squeezing her biceps tighter. "No, I'm not. At least, I'm not unless I get the signal."

"Oh, your sister lets it ring and then hangs up and then calls you back?"

"Yes."

Cameron walked to the front door. He sighed heavily before opening it. "Tell Jennifer that I need to see her."

Cameron closed the door on the way out and hurried to his car. He had thirty minutes before he was supposed to meet with Evian. But before he met Evian he stopped and made a call to Vance. They did a quick story swap and revealed everything they had learned.

Cameron was five minutes late when he drove into the driveway of James Evian. Two bodyguards met Cameron at the door, frisked him, and escorted him to Evian's main den. The furniture was oriental. As a boy Evian was reared in New York City. His mother was born in Japan. She lived her first twenty years in Tokyo before she moved to New York and married James' father.

Evian was very short man with a blend of oriental features. He was brought up on the poor side of New York. He had seen it all. To him there was death, and then, there was painful death. James expanded his operation from the New York loan market to the practically virgin territory of Atlanta. He quickly established his reputation for being pitiless and enjoying the pain of others. Within a few months he became the chief loan shark in Atlanta.

When Cameron entered the room, he had a quick flash back to the first time he met with Evian. It was over a year ago when Cameron happened to arrive while Evian was hosting a it special occasion. They were celebrating a man named 'Big Ron" and his advancement into a leadership role with the mob. Big Ron would be reporting directly to Evian. He gave Big Ron a gold ring with a jeweled globe on it. Only a dozen people could wear this ring. Big Ron's dad wore this particular one until he died. Cameron wanted to arrest Evian and his hoods back then, but the FBI quickly notified him to stay away.

Cameron did what the FBI asked of him, until tonight.

Tonight did nothing but bring back bad memories. Cameron listened as Evian announced the entertainment for the evening. The highlight of the night was a special fight. Evian liked winners who were underestimated and considered underdogs. He backed a gorgeous oriental woman who specialized in kickboxing. She was slender, petite and on first appearance didn't seem tough enough to last half a round. She was too beautiful to be tough. Once a week Evian would entertain his guests with a good fight. There were no rules. No time limit. No equipment. And only he could stop a fight.

Evian's bodyguard showed Cameron to a seat. The two women fighters were brought into the room simultaneously and told that it was a fight to the finish. The winner would receive $1,000. The unusually beautiful oriental woman was nicknamed Butterfly.

Actually, the fight wasn't even close. Within seconds Butterfly had penetrated her tall opponent's slapping offense and landed a couple of hard rights to her opponent's chin. After two more blows, the tall woman crumbled to her knees. Butterfly then kicked her in the face so hard that it flattened her immediately. She jumped on the woman's back and pulled her hair backward viciously. It was clearly painful.

Evian was all smiles. He cheered for Butterfly to be cruel. In turn, Butterfly put more pressure on her opponent's leg making the tall woman scream in pain.

"Yes." Evian shouted. He stood up and shook his fist in the air. "Come on Butterfly! Come on!"

"Eight, nine, ten." Evian counted loudly. He then threw his hand up to halt the fight.

Butterfly stopped on command. She stood up and walked proudly around the room. The guests were cheering. Everyone was caught in the glory. Everyone cheered loudly except Cameron. He watched as a few of the bodyguards dragged the tall woman away.

Evian gave Butterfly her prize purse and then kissed her. She was sweating and breathing hard but her opponent didn't make a mark on her. She didn't even break a fingernail. Her beauty remained untouched. After Evian returned to his seat he looked at Cameron. "Well, Lieutenant, what do you think of my entertainment?"

Cameron studied Evian. He looked five feet tall with a clearly defined widow's peak in his hairline. Evian always wore dark sunglasses. Day or night he wore sunglasses.

"I think it's exactly what I would expect from someone like you."

"Oh?" Evian's eyes narrowed as he leaned forward. "And, just what does that mean?"

Cameron knew that he better back off. "I figured that a man like you would surround yourself with exceptional beauty, strength and talent."

A broad smile crossed Evian's face as he leaned back into his chair. He pointed to Big Ron, "Speaking of talent someday that man will take my place." Evian said this like a proud father.

Cameron didn't study Big Ron long instead he turned to more pressing matters. "I'm here about Robert Lancaster."

"A most unfortunate accident." Evian sighed without true care.

Cameron checked the positions of Evian's bodyguards. One on each side of him and three others by the doorway. If things got nasty Cameron would have only one option. He would have to get his hands on Evian.

"Rumor has it that Lancaster owed you a great deal of money." Cameron stated flatly.

"You think that I decided to collect in an alternative fashion?"

Cameron kept his eye on the guard who was located at Evian's left. He at least looked the weaker of the two. "Something like that."

"Well, tell me, Lieutenant," Evian waived his short thick arms around the room. "Did you not see how I receive my pleasure in life?"

"Yes, I did."

"And what did you see, Lieutenant?"

"I saw a woman in pain."

"Precisely!" Evian shouted. "So, why do you think that I would let a man, who was hot with the fever, off so easily as to push him out the window. Really, Lieutenant, you disappoint me."

Cameron figured the fight had a purpose. If nothing else to remind him of the type of man he had come to see. No, it was very unlikely that Evian would let Robert Lancaster off so easily.

"Besides, Lancaster got lucky last week." Evian turned to his guest. "Imagine, the man won ten overs and three unders and beat ten spreads."

"I thought he owed you a small fortune."

"He did, but he was paying it off." Evian stood up. "I liked doing business with Lancaster. He always found a way to pay. I'd be a fool to lose him as a customer."

"How much remains on his debt?"

"A lot."

"So you'll lose on this one?"

"No, I never do business without collateral." Evian smiled, "I'll get his house."

Sitting down, Cameron was almost eye level with Evian. "Does Lancaster's wife know?"

Evian laughed. "Oh, really, Lieutenant, I'm not totally without heart. I'm going to let his widow at least bury the man."

Cameron waited for the punch line.

"I wouldn't think of moving her out on the streets until... At least, after the weekend."

"That's big of you."

A second loud crack of laughter barreled through the room followed by a sudden silence. "In fact, Lieutenant, if I ever catch the dog that nailed Lancaster, I will personally demand satisfaction for the remainder of his debt."

Cameron was escorted out the same way he came in. It was past midnight.

CHAPTER 12

ATLANTA, GEORGIA
JUNE 2001

IT WAS the middle of the afternoon and Quincy had a meeting with Vance in twenty minutes. Quincy learned to be early for meetings. He was scheduled to hear the latest about their subcommittee efforts. He knew that Vance handpicked half a dozen medical professionals for their input and that the CIS woman would be stopping by any day now. The possibilities were unlimited. Everyday his excitement soared. Everyday he thought about it. Quincy tagged the marble entrance sign in front of Greystone Hospital and started to trot up the steps when he saw a familiar face.

The man was Quincy's buddy from his old neighborhood who worked at Greystone as an orderly. They played baseball together when they were kids. Occasionally they saw each other around the hospital and talked about old times. They always talked in slang. A poetic play on words. A secret code that reflected their uniqueness. His full nickname was M Daddy. He grew a mustache during his teens and he always had plenty of women, thus the daddy part.

Quincy stopped in his tracks and walked over to the small group.

"What's happenin'?" Quincy asked spiritedly.

M Daddy put his arm around one of the women. "It's all good."

Quincy looked at his friend's young girlfriend and noticed her colorful clothes and long fingernails. Her fingernails sparkled with glitter.

"Come on, my man," M Daddy emphasized that he wanted Quincy to come by the old hood and visit him again. "When will you ever come around the way, man?"

Quincy pointed at him as he backed up. "Hey, I plan to come to the hood soon." To Quincy that was like saying, 'let's do lunch'.

"Yeah, sure ya will." M Daddy was quick to fire back, "You just scared man. Now that you're a big baller and all freshly dipped, you're worried that the girls will all be sweatin' ya now."

Quincy gave a short laugh, as he had to translate the slang himself. He was no longer fluent in slang 101. He knew that 'big baller' was a nickname for someone who had become successful and that 'freshly dipped' was code for a sharp new suit and tie. 'Sweatin' just meant that the women would be chasing him for marriage.

"No, road dog," Quincy replied with the familiar slang that someone used to refer to a close friend, "more like I've probably lost my stripes around the old hood."

Quincy was still thinking about his old neighborhood and how times had changed when he looked into Vance's office. Uncharacteristically Vance had left his door open. When Quincy peered into the room he could see Vance talking to someone.

Vance waived for him to enter.

After a few steps into the doorway Quincy could see the lines of a beautiful blonde. She was wearing a conservative dark blue pants suit, but it didn't conceal all of her qualities.

Vance introduced Quincy to the CIS specialist who had been assigned to their subcommittee. Her name is Pamela Reed.

Quincy felt nervous for the first time in a long while. Maybe, it was the realization that the subcommittee was on the brink of starting.

Maybe, it was seeing Pamela. A strikingly beautiful woman. A real diamond in his old friend M Daddy's lingo.

Their eyes met and stayed locked for more than a casual moment.

Vance looked at the two of them. He observed them in a distant way. Both seemed a little awkward. Both seemed to be trying to hide their first impressions. Neither was successful.

"So," Vance spoke up abruptly. "Ms. Reed…"

"Please," Pamela interrupted, "let's not be so formal… just call me Pamela."

Vance nodded his agreement as he leaned back in his chair. He was reviewing Pamela's resume.

He opened the folder. "It says here that you have a graduate degree in computer science from Mississippi State. Over the last six years you have worked with Vice President Lancaster, who we all know is the President's chief advisor."

Of course, the entire resume was bogus. Senator Adams had his men create the false history of Pamela. Neil Henry was behind it all and had even used his leverage to coerce the agreement from the Vice President.

Pamela brushed a small piece of string off her pants. "I like working in politics." She slowly crossed her legs toward Quincy. "I find it rewarding to try and influence the way our political leaders think."

"You like influencing the decision making processes?" Vance asked.

"Yes, good decisions must be based on good information." Pamela spoke softly. "And that's what I do. I gather information and present it in a way that it will make sense to people. Then they can rationally decide the best course to follow."

"I think I could say the same about you, Doctor." She was talking to Quincy. I'm sure you like to influence the decision makers or you wouldn't be on this subcommittee." Pamela had received a list of team members from Vance the week before.

She spoke from memory. "You got your medical degree from

Morehouse School of Medicine. You have a double major from undergraduate school in archeology and psychology." Pamela picked up her pace. "You had a 3.8 average from college and a 3.7 in medical school. You apparently loved sports because you were a baseball player throughout college. You are somewhat social because you were a member of a fraternity. And...."

Quincy was very impressed. "And?"

"And, doctor..."

"Please, call me Quincy."

"Ok, Quincy." Pamela stated cleverly, "you're single."

Quincy looked back at Vance. "I'd say she has done her homework."

Vance's left eye squinted as he listened to Pamela talk. "Well, there are different kinds of information, but..."

"I would think you would have a great appreciation for objective information gathering." Pamela interrupted.

"Oh, I do. But objective information doesn't live in a vacuum. There is a context, a story if you will that helps us interpret information. The problem is that many people cannot collect or deal with subjective information because their own emotions get in the way." He looked at Quincy. "That's why it's important that you learn how to observe rather than just look— how to focus on a subject so intensely that your emotional turmoil doesn't prevent you from making accurate observations."

Vance looked at his watch. "Unfortunately, I have to run now. I'm sure Quincy can show you around a bit if you like."

Pamela stood up and shook Vance's hand. "Thank you for your time, doctor."

Vance let the word "doctor" linger without correction. He didn't like the new informal business approach. It didn't go unnoticed by Pamela.

"I assume, doctor," Pamela continued, "that we will start having regular meetings."

"Actually," Vance gave it a few seconds of thought. "I can't start until 8:30 and we might as well start tomorrow. We'll decide then how often we need to meet."

Pamela pulled out her Palm Pilot and entered their meeting time. Quincy led her slowly down the hall. He was in no rush.

WASHINGTON, D.C.
JUNE 2001

Senator Adams was in his limo when he got the call from Pamela. She gave him a full update. She was particularly proud of her ability to recite the resume that had been created for her, along with the resumes of Dr. Watts and Dr. Connelly. The Catfish liked to hear a good story. He also liked to know that his plan was working. He wanted Pamela to go into complete detail about Quincy. During her tour around Greystone, Pamela had found out a lot about the handsome Dr. Watts. She hoped that he was susceptible to her influences. For the most part she discovered that Quincy was up to his pretty brown eyeballs in debt.

Quincy got an academic scholarship for college and medical school, but he had borrowed a lot of money to help his grandmother live in a decent assisted living center. Ever since Quincy's parents died, he assumed full responsibility for his grandmother. She was still alive and well and the debt just kept growing. A few weeks ago his grandmother needed an outpatient procedure on her feet, but her HMO refused to pay for it. The HMO administrator told the doctor that the procedure was cosmetic and not really necessary. Quincy laughed at that one. If she didn't have the procedure she could not walk because of severe pain. The administrator argued that Quincy wanted to put his grandmother through a cosmetic procedure just so her feet would look good and the HMO stuck to its guns.

The Catfish even laughed at that story. "Ok, so we have an angle on Quincy. Did anything surface on Connelly's number one man?"

"I assume," Pamela inquired, "you're referring to Bill Barringer as his number one man?"

"Of course."

"No, I haven't met him yet."

"And how about the big dog?"

"You mean, Connelly?"

"Yes." The senator continued. "How is my old nemesis?"

"I'll be on their computer system soon and I'll be able to dig deeper on Connelly."

The senator hung up with a quick goodbye. His limo driver pulled up to a curb where a man had been waiting. The man had been waiting for over thirty minutes. The Senator always liked to be the one in control by making his stooges wait for him. He liked flexing his power. There had been a light rain all day so the man was well hidden under an umbrella. As they pulled up to the curb, the senator cracked his window and told Larry Colburn to hop into the limo.

A strong gust of wind and misty rain shot through the door as Colburn entered the limo.

Colburn was meeting with the senator before heading to Atlanta. They decided to choose a place that was more private than their last lunch meeting.

As soon as Colburn got into the car the senator started talking. "Well, did you get the money?"

"Yes," Colburn was wiping the moisture off of his face and hands.

The Catfish handed Colburn a small towel with an embroidered Mississippi State seal and flag. Colburn passed the towel back to the senator without bothering to use it. "Let's get on with our business, Senator."

The senator tossed the towel on the floor. "Here is a folder containing documents about all of the main players."

Colburn opened the folder and saw a picture of Vance Connelly, several newspaper articles from the last time Connelly was involved with the Senate hearings and a resume. He looked through the pictures. Quincy's picture was in the folder.

"Does this guy work with Connelly?" Colburn asked.

"Yes. He's an intern at the hospital, but according to my source, he is taking some time off to join forces with the health commission."

The wheels were already turning in Colburn's mind.

"How long do I have before I get things into the court?" Colburn asked.

"It's all timing." The senator pulled out one of his many fine cigars but didn't light it. He just rolled it between his thumb and forefinger and inhaled its aroma. "I want a good story to break around mid to late September."

"It usually takes me about two or three months to really cause chaos. Then it may take several years before it hits the court."

"I don't care about the actual court trial." Senator Adams pulled out a lighter to heat his cigar. "But I do care about stirring up a fuss inside Greystone Hospital and getting a lot of exposure in the news. And, I need that to happen in September." The senator intentionally repeated the month for Colburn's benefit.

Colburn had no trouble understanding. "And if I'm on time and do a really good job..?"

"If you do this one right, I'll bump your initial retainer 40%." The senator hated bartering sessions. Everybody tried to squeeze more money.

Colburn seemed pleased as he tucked the file under his coat and without saying anything else, without even a glimpse back at the senator, he opened the door and got out of the car.

The Catfish watched as Colburn disappeared in the misty rain. Soon his limo would be filled with the sweet smell of a Cuban cigar. He had decided to light the magnificent cigar right away.

CHAPTER 13

ATLANTA, GEORGIA
JUNE 2001

QUINCY LIVED in a small stucco condo in North Highlands, a small, eclectic community of Atlanta. It had one bedroom tacked onto a living room, a tiny kitchen that barely allowed the use of a small table and a chair. There was no air conditioning and he had to build his own shower to fit the cast iron tub in the bathroom. Quincy liked the size of his condo, if for nothing else than it was easy to clean. Besides, he didn't spend enough time there to feel claustrophobic and the condo had character. Anyway, as an intern he spent most of his time at Greystone and paid very little rent for his condo.

Quincy's favorite bars were only a stone's throw away from his condo. A short pleasant walk. He usually got a chance to visit his stomping grounds once, maybe twice a month; preferably on a Saturday night if he didn't have to go to work at Greystone at dawn the next day. He'd start at the Highland Tap with a gin martini, their specialty, watch the diverse mid-town crowd for a while and then order a large house-aged New York Strip. He liked his steak Philadelphia style, charred crispy on the outside, and pink and juicy on the inside.

He loved the big slices of mushroom, sautéed in butter with just a hint of tarragon piled atop his steak. He opted for the roasted garlic mashed Yukon Gold potato with a dash of Worcestershire sauce and butter whisked in; simple but profoundly satisfying.

Quincy had just ordered his first gin martini at The Tap when Larry Colburn sat down next to him. Colburn was also about to work on a martini, but his was made with premium Russian spirits.

"Stoli, straight up, hold the vermouth and toss in an extra olive." Colburn said with an air of assuredness.

Three sips later and Colburn was ready to slip into a conversation with Quincy. He had been waiting for the right moment. The perfect opportunity came when two beautiful young women stepped up to the bar to get their drinks and then disappeared back into the crowd.

Colburn leaned over toward Quincy, "Is it always like this?"

Quincy raised his eyebrows as if to answer, "Like what?"

Colburn looked around briefly, "This is my kind of place. Didn't you see those women that were just standing here?"

"I saw 'em." Quincy knew them. "Give it up, they're gay."

Colburn's eyes showed his surprise before he turned his head for a second look.

This was the type of event that made it easy to start up a conversation. Quincy angled himself so that he could study Colburn closer. He couldn't help but notice Colburn's clean shaven head, pearl white teeth, light brown skin and deep voice. They exchanged brief introductions, a hardy handshake and the usual background chit chat of two strangers. Where are you from? How long have you been here? Have you ever eaten here before?

The whole time they were talking Colburn was thinking about his deal with Senator Adams. How he snooped around Greystone to find good candidates for their scheme. How he reviewed everything he could about the people and history of Greystone. How he measured his timetable to meet those he planned to incorporate in his scheme. Quincy was among the first.

Soon their conversation came to the next standard question, "What do you do for a living?"

"I'm a lawyer, Quincy." Colburn's eyes brightened as he started to talk a little shop.

"Do you have some legal action around here?"

"Will have."

Quincy nodded and asked the bartender for another drink.

Colburn pulled out a substantial roll of bills and paid for the drink. "It's on me, Quincy."

"Thanks, but lawyers don't usually buy doctors a drink."

"Doctor?" Colburn acted as if he didn't know that Quincy was a physician.

"Actually, I'm a medical intern at Greystone."

"That's not too shabby."

"You seem like a nice guy Colburn, but I can tell you now that your profession and mine don't mix."

Colburn could see that this sort of topic could sour his plan to become friends with Quincy. He decided to change the topic. "So, what, uh, made you decide to go to Greystone?"

"Opportunity. The kind of opportunity that can make a career." Quincy didn't mind talking about himself. But, now that he knew Colburn was a lawyer he raised his guard a bit.

"I bet it's got to be hard over there."

Quincy's food arrived. He figured he'd eat and then head over to a jazz bar. "Hard? Sure it's hard. But what do you expect from one of the best in the country? They work my butt off and it's not like I make the big dough."

"No," Colburn realized that Quincy misunderstood him. "I mean, 'hard' because you're an African-American trying to work your way through a white man's system."

"Oh, that kind of hard." Quincy acknowledged. "Sometimes."

"Come on now. Do you think you get the same deal as the rest of them?"

"So far I haven't had any problems."

"Yeah, I'm sure they're real fair folks. I bet that's why they always wear those starchy white coats everywhere, right? In the old days they probably wore big pointed white hats with a hood to cover their faces, too."

Quincy was getting more and more irritated. "Why are you dragging this stuff up, man?"

"Because I think there could be some travesty of injustice lingering around over there."

Quincy took a bite of steak and chewed it slowly to calm himself. "And you believe this because…?"

"Don't make me laugh, man." Colburn shook his head as if Quincy had been hoodwinked. "Where there is a wood pile, there are usually snakes." Colburn pushed, "So, what doctor over there do you know that has ever helped our cause?"

Forking another bite of steak and then scooping up a bite of mashed potatoes, Quincy took his time chewing. He washed it down with some water. He never liked to drink alcohol when he was eating. In fact, dinner was usually his cue for stopping the high-octane stuff for the evening.

"The man I'm thinking of is my mentor," Quincy said confidently, "and his name is Vance Connelly."

Colburn already had studied the files on Connelly. He knew that Connelly had been there in the early days. He knew that he was well known in his field. What he didn't know about Connelly were things that weren't written down but were folklore around Greystone. "And what did Connelly do?"

Quincy calmly ate a few more bites before he decided that he wasn't enjoying this conversation. It had killed his appetite. Quincy slid his unfinished plate to the front of the bar. He asked for a tab from the waiter before he continued his little discussion with Colburn. "Well, he was a player in those early days of integration."

"So he was part of that old era and was probably…"

"Don't jump to any conclusions." Quincy picked up his bill, examined it for a second and then handed the waiter his credit card.

While he waited to sign the receipt Quincy explained about Vance. How Vance, as long as he has been with Greystone, had also worked with Grady Hospital, the Atlanta public hospital. In fact he was chief of medicine there. He personally pushed a wheelchair occupied by a black patient from one side of Grady to the white side of the hospital when the integration process was mandated by law. This was a first for Grady. Quincy also pointed out that Vance appointed the first African-American chief resident of medicine at Grady. The facts were adding up, but not in Colburns favor.

Quincy added a tip to his bill and put away his credit card. "A lot of people were worried about what would happen the day they integrated the hospital. You know they feared that someone would do something irrational. There was a lot of fear. But you know what?"

Colburn remained silent.

"Vance Connelly told everyone on the medical service that things would be fine, and he was right."

Quincy decided he didn't like Colburn. He waived good-bye to the waiter and then stood up tall. "You know, Mr. Colburn, I have a funny feeling our meeting was not by chance. Who wants you to stir the pot down here and why? Because I can tell you now, I'm at Greystone everyday and I don't see any discrimination."

Colburn didn't respond, he simply took another sip of his martini.

WASHINGTON, D.C.
JUNE 2001

Triplett stared at the surface of the shiny marble conference table that extended twenty feet across the room. He enjoyed examining the intricate design of the various colors of marble. Each piece came from a different country. Italian marble was his favorite. He was waiting patiently for his six o'clock meeting with the CEO's of three major generic brand pharmaceutical firms and Senator Adams. The Catfish was there because Triplett told him to be there. Adam's presence gave support to Triplett's plan. They had to scratch each other's back. Triplett maintained this high profile office only five blocks away from the capitol. The CEO's were flying to Washington from their various locations for a short meeting.

It was 6:15 p.m. before they were all settled around the end of the table. Fresh coffee was served by Triplett's secretary. She smiled and leaned forward generously with each pour. Triplett figured that she would be the right icebreaker for this crowd. He was right. They were all stirred and ready to talk business.

Triplett began.

The youngest of the CEO's, who had just turned 41, was quick to interject. "I don't know about you gentlemen, but I read the proposal that Triplett offered our company very carefully and I find it to be totally ridiculous and offensive."

The other CEO's nodded their heads in agreement.

"I thought it was a very generous offer." Triplett said with his deep raspy voice.

"According to your proposal," the young CEO explained, "we have two actions to discuss."

He had started taking over the meeting. "The first is a 50 million dollar offer for a two-year delay in creating the generic drugs that will compete with your brand drugs like Jorestat -2."

"Correct," Triplett confirmed. "The patents are about to expire on three of the drugs that interest us. By delaying the creation of the generic drugs the brand-names can continue to be sold at their current price. Speck MediSurge will pay you to do that." Triplett figured that Speck MediSurge would make back the money plus a good profit in one business year. "The point is—you don't have any risk in the deal."

"Yes, we understand that." The young CEO spoke in a clipped

New England accent. "The second action is about your newly developed drugs that will be patented for a number of years so we in the generic field can't touch them." The young CEO had little patience and he spoke in short bursts. "You want to allow us access to these drugs a year or so before the patents expire. In fact you will pay us to do that."

Triplett could see that this CEO was going to be a headache.

The young CEO raised his index finger into the air to make one more point. "That is, if we will sell our generic brand for only a 5% discount instead of the 40% to 50% discount we usually provide."

"That is correct as well." Triplett thought the plans brought possibilities that were reasonable and allowed for a dual moneymaking strategy. This was the carrot in the deal. He also knew that the advertising capability of Speck MediSurge would crush the little companies that made the generics.

An older more seasoned CEO with neatly groomed white hair and distinguished looking face spoke. "I believe we will be targets of lawsuits from the government if we try this kind of deception."

Another older CEO who had dyed his hair too black for his skin color also chimed into the conversation. "Not to mention the consumer groups that will start filing class-action suits."

Senator Adams had been fiddling with a nice Cuban cigar and was listening to their fears. "Gentlemen," he offered in a calm collected manner, "Triplett is not asking you to do anything illegal. He's simply trying to find methods to ensure the future profits of your firms."

"What?" The young CEO had an outraged tone in his voice.

The senator continued with his thoughts. "The cost of creating new pharmaceuticals is going through the roof."

They all agreed to the obvious.

"Well, in the long run if you continue down the current path you will be putting each other out of business. The senator rolled his cigar between his thumb and fingers. "You guys need the big name-brands to forge ahead with new research so that you can clone their products so your companies will not be stuck with the cost of the initial research."

The room was heavy with thoughtful silence.

"In addition," Triplett sat up straight towering over the CEO's and the senator. "Your stockholders will be very happy."

The younger CEO stood up and looked around the room. "What you are suggesting here is wrong and I want nothing to do with it. I also believe that instead of helping us, it will destroy our companies. The cost of generic drugs to the patients will sky-rocket and public trust will dive."

Pulling out his cell phone the younger CEO announced to the group that he was calling his pilot and telling him to start warming up the engines to his company jet. This meeting was over as far as he was concerned. Triplett kept his eye on him as he stormed out of the room.

There was a short lull before Triplett put his offer on the table to the other CEO's. "Well, gentlemen, now that we got Mr. Conscience out of the room, how do you feel about making a lot of money for your firms?"

The black haired man spoke up softly. "My firm is not a non-profit organization. We are in business to make money and I for one will be happy to endorse your proposal, Mr. Triplett."

The other CEO was quick to confirm the deal as well.

The senator offered the others a cigar. Only Triplett accepted the offer as they all remained around the table and worked out the details of their agreement. Triplett and the Senator would find other means to convince the younger CEO. Perhaps he would have some IRS complication, or even a hostile takeover of his firm. Actually, Triplett could easily buy enough shares of the young CEO's company and in a snap, Triplett would be in charge of another drug manufacturing plant. Then it would be business as usual. Another example made. If worse came to worse, perhaps a painful experience with a lost family member. After all the young CEO did have several children that he loved deeply.

CHAPTER 14

ATLANTA, GEORGIA
OCTOBER 1952

LOOKING OUT the window, the sky appeared clear, and the moonlight was strong again this morning. Vance was struggling to sit comfortably in his thinking chair. The chair felt stiff and awkward and he was fidgeting and adjusting his body. Nothing seemed to fit. His scheduled time for thinking should have ended an hour ago. But he knew that his mind wouldn't let him proceed to his next phase. Writing on a manuscript was out of the question this morning and he wasn't going to waste his time trying.

On the surface everything related to the Robert Lancaster case seemed to have an explanation, but some details didn't fall into place. Like an off centered painting, the details of the case were just plain annoying to Vance. He stroked his morning stubble. Yes, the details. The lieutenant, Cameron, caught one of them. Nurses never called patients by their first name. At least, Vance didn't think so.

The bolts on the window. Could they have been loosened by someone who had been lightly sedated? Perhaps. And then there was Wasserman's relationship with Robert Lancaster. It was not all that unusual, but then again, why didn't Wasserman tell the Lieutenant that he was a friend of Lancaster?

Those damn details. Why did Jennifer Eden have to take a vacation? She had seen death many times before this.

Vance was still staring out the window when the newspaper flew up his driveway. He walked briskly down his driveway in his bathrobe and slippers. He usually waited until the evening when he could sit back and enjoy a glass of wine and casually read the paper. Today he wanted to know what the press was saying about the Robert Lancaster case. He marched back to the house and spread the paper out on the kitchen table. The only thing that he could find was a small article on the eighth page of Section A. It was a simple announcement stating that the cause of the fall was still under investigation and that the funeral was to be at Patterson's Funeral Home at 11:00 today.

It was mid-morning and Vance and Cameron had a scheduled meeting. They bumped into each other at the elevator and started heading toward Vance's office. Just before they reached his destination, Vance stopped to listen to a group of nurses chatting. The two men stood in silence.

At first Cameron thought that Vance was waiting to talk to one of the nurses. But Vance had that opportunity when a nurse parted the group and walked pass them. Vance said nothing. Cameron wondered what Vance was up to. Now he was listening in on a nurse talking about a patient. Finally, Vance broke away and proceeded to his office.

Vance brewed some coffee and poured two cups. Cameron smiled and finally broke the ice. "Why were we standing out in the hallway like that?"

Vance was pleased that Cameron waited until now to ask. "I was listening to the nurses and how they talk about their patients."

Cameron mulled over the reply for a minute. "And what did you discover?"

Vance smiled, "The purpose was to see if nurses were calling their patients by their first name."

Cameron took another sip of coffee. The coffee tasted bitter and had a strong bite. It didn't seem to faze Vance; he even appeared to like it that way. Cameron cleared his throat. "I don't think I heard the nurses do that."

"No, I didn't hear a single nurse use a first name." Vance agreed.

Vance finished his coffee and poured a second cup. "I've gone over the records on Robert Lancaster a number of times."

"Anything new?" Cameron inquired.

"No, not yet."

Cameron sighed heavily. "Well, I'm hitting a few dead ends myself."

"You look worn out, Lieutenant."

Cameron didn't bother to shave that morning and he had hardly slept. Most of the night he paced the floor thinking about his visit to James Evian. What a sick son of a bitch that man was.

Cameron gave the details to Vance. He even included the story of how he first met Evian. He told Vance about the celebration of Big Ron's elevation in the pecking order of the mob a year ago and how the FBI told him to stay clear. Cameron described the mob cult and how they reflected their rank with a precious globe jeweled ring. Then Cameron told Vance the highlights of his most recent meeting, including the fight. He wanted Vance to know the sort of low life people he had to associate with to get to the bottom of a case.

Vance leaned back in his chair and looked at the ceiling as he thought aloud, "It sounds like Robert Lancaster wasn't under any pressure from the loan shark or the bookies?"

"None."

"And you feel confident that this Mr. Evian had nothing to do with it?"

"A loan shark doesn't knock off his best paying customer. Besides the man wouldn't have let Lancaster off so easily."

Suddenly Vance sat up straight and rubbed his chin. "Maybe we're on the wrong side of the equation." Vance stopped rubbing his chin. His face reflected his insight. "You see, we've been thinking in terms of Lancaster being in trouble. We guessed that the turmoil of his depression drove him to jump."

"I don't think I ever really believed that one." Cameron stated.

"No, it never sat right with me either. Then, we both figured that Lancaster must have been in so much trouble that someone wanted to watch him suffer."

"That's still a possibility."

Vance held up two fingers to match the number of theories. "A third option," Vance held up a third finger, "is that Lancaster was punishing someone else. Perhaps he was causing enough trouble for someone that it was motive enough for that person to kill him."

Cameron pondered what Vance said. "Discounting the first option of suicide that leaves us with a murder."

"Are you going to announce that to the press?"

"No, I want whoever is guilty of this, to think that we're sold on the notion that it was suicide."

Vance was thinking of the repercussion for the hospital. "I take it that we can pursue this delicately."

Cameron didn't bother to answer instead he reached into his pocket and pulled out the pictures that he had confiscated from Jennifer's place. He never had told Vance about taking the film without a warrant. He spread a few of the photos out on the table.

Somehow Vance figured he didn't want to know how his partner got the photos. Vance studied them closely. He noticed the date printed on the corner of one of the pictures indicating that they were taken during spring of this year.

Vance ran through the photos until he hit one that struck him. It was a picture of Jennifer standing on a balcony. She had a smile across her face. The wind had blown her hair partially across her face. She was holding a small replica of a sailing ship. A world class racing yacht. Like those in the World Cup.

Vance changed the conversation quickly. "So, what's your plan now?"

Cameron gathered up the photos. "I plan to get a good night sleep for a change."

As soon as Cameron left the room, Vance asked his secretary to get Robert Lancaster's office on the phone. Shortly, Vance was talking to Lancaster's former executive assistant. She sounded like a woman under a deadline. Vance told her who he was and that he had to complete some of Lancaster's records. Clearly she didn't have the time or the inclination to talk to Vance. The good news was that she did agree to meet with him. She planned a working lunch and would give him a few minutes.

Robert Lancaster's office complex was in a high rise in the middle of Atlanta. The building was completed in 1951 and was one of the tallest of the era. Walters, Lancaster, Smith and Associates was on the top floor of the building.

Vance opened the oak doors and was immediately greeted by a receptionist. She never lost her picture perfect smile as she led him to Lancaster's old office. Lancaster's former executive assistant would join him shortly.

Vance sat in one of the many chairs and assessed the office. The main desk was massive and made of cherry oak. The executive chair was covered with red leather giving it an air of power. There was a striking portrait centered on the wall behind the desk of a woman dressed in a white gown. A large, heavily jeweled, necklace and matching bracelet caught his eye. Vance stood up and admired the portrait. Strong and, yes, even regal. Her features, however, were dark. She had black hair and a dark tan. She could be Spanish.

"I see that you are among the many who admire that portrait." A woman's voice slid across the room. "It's of Mrs. Lancaster."

Vance turned around to see a woman walking toward him. She had brunette hair, bright red lipstick and wore a conservative dress. She introduced herself as Lancaster's former assistant.

She motioned to the sitting area. "You've got a few minutes of my time, Doctor."

"I'll get straight to the point then." Vance figured that Lancaster didn't advertise his gambling habit. "Did he ever complain about his…?"

"His heart condition, Doctor?"

"Yes. At least he must have said—"

"No, he never complained about his heart."

"I know that the nature of his work made him travel a lot." Vance stated.

"That is the beast of the business as he used to say."

"Was he tired?"

She crossed her legs. "I don't know any of the businessmen around here who aren't tired from travel."

"Was he on the road more than usual this month?"

She nodded her confirmation.

"Any place particular?"

"Charleston." She was checking her watch. "He had so much business in Charleston over the last few years that the company bought a condo for him there." She checked her watch once again. "Now really I don't see how this is helping you. Besides I'm not supposed to talk about Mr. Lancaster's business life."

"Well, I just need…"

She stood up. "I'm afraid, Doctor Connelly, that your time is up."

Vance checked his own watch. The time had gone fast. It didn't take much of Vance's analytical prowess to quickly diagnose her aggressive Type A personality. She was definitely time-urgent and had the propensity to interrupt conversations. As Vance started to stand he noticed a framed picture on the credenza. It was a picture of a balcony overlooking the ocean. He stopped in front of the picture.

"Doctor, please, I must get back to work."

"Sure." Vance pointed to the picture. "Where is this?"

"Doctor, your time is up and I don't want to talk anymore."

Vance took a second look at the picture. Vance figured he could squeeze a little more information from her.

"It's in the city of…" Vance stopped abruptly.

"Charleston." She said impatiently as she tried to escort him toward the door.

"Really?"

She waived her hand toward the door.

"I think I've been there, it looks like the…"

"The Sand Dune."

"Right!" Vance smiled, pleased with himself for extracting from her what he needed despite her controlling and rude behavior. He enjoyed a slow stroll out the door.

On the way down the elevator, Vance knew that he had to fly to Charleston. The scene in the photograph looked identical to the photograph that Cameron had shown him earlier. The only difference was that Jennifer was in Cameron's photo.

It was late and Cameron wasn't going to get one of those good nights sleep he promised himself. He must have checked his rear view mirror a thousand times. A black Ford was hanging tough. Well, the hell with it. Let the brutes follow him. He figured it was Evian's men at work. He drove down Peachtree, turned right on Lindberg and then took a left on Doran Avenue. The Ford stayed glued to his every turn.

As he pulled into the paved circular driveway, Cameron admired the Lancaster's colonial brick home. The front yard was meticulously manicured and inviting. Cameron wondered if Victoria Lancaster had the capital to pay Evian. He looked over his shoulder to make sure that his favorite Bozo's were in sight. They were.

Cameron rang the bell and was greeted by Victoria Lancaster. She was wearing a beautiful low-cut dress as if she was expecting company. She was about five feet nine inches tall and in her early forties.

Cameron explained who he was and why he was there.

Mrs. Lancaster's smile sent a rush of adrenaline throughout Cameron's body.

She moved gracefully into the den. "I was just about to sit down and read the paper, Lieutenant." Her voice was both soft and raspy, a blend of English and Spanish.

"I've been meaning to come by." Cameron was searching for what to say next. "I wanted to give you a chance to absorb everything."

"Actually, Lieutenant, I really wasn't too surprised."

"You weren't?"

"No." Victoria Lancaster leaned forward to reach for the glass of water sitting on the marble coffee table in front of them. "Robert had tried to commit suicide before."

Cameron's jaw dropped at least an inch. In that one instant just when he thought that he was making headway, Victoria made the suicide option viable again. "I haven't seen any reports that would indicate that your husband had tried to take his own life."

"Of course not, Lieutenant." Victoria was sitting with her hands lightly folded in her lap.

"How did he keep his medical records so clean?"

"Really, Lieutenant. Can you imagine telling the public that he was emotionally unstable? Remember he dealt with large sums of money. That is dangerous information that would have ruined him and his family business."

Cameron was still trying to absorb what she was telling him.

She purred a soft laugh. "Robert made sure that it remained a secret. He paid a good bit to keep his medical problems confidential."

Cameron was feeling that warm surge up his spine again as Victoria reached for her glass again with her long, delicate fingers.

She sipped the water without losing eye contact.

"So tell me, how did he try to commit suicide?" Cameron inquired.

"He planned everything to the finest detail." She had a reflective look in her eye. "He made a visit to his lawyer and got his will in order. Then, he waited until after our wedding anniversary in May. He always loved that time of year." She thought for a moment, "Then he sent me on a trip to a health spa in the Greek Isles. It was such a beautiful place."

"Tell me, did he leave a suicide note?"

"Yes, it was a short note that seemed very confusing. It mostly talked about how depressed he was."

Cameron nodded for her to continue with her story.

"While I was gone he drank a bottle of Vodka and took half a dozen sleeping pills. He went to the garage and started his car."

"He tried carbon monoxide poisoning?"

"Yes." She took a sip of water.

"That sounds like it could have done the job. What happened?"

"He got too sick to finish."

Cameron raked his hand through his hair. "You must have been devastated."

Victoria Lancaster looked deeply into Cameron's eyes. "To tell you the truth, Lieutenant, Robert and I had an arranged marriage."

"Robert was on a business trip in my country." Victoria smiled at the memory. "I was his interpreter."

"And he fell in love with you?"

"Yes, all he had to do was to make a financial arrangement with my father."

"You mean he bought you?"

She brushed her hair back from her face. "Don't be so naive, Lieutenant, he gave my father more money than he could have made in twenty years. In exchange, I married Robert." She smiled.

Cameron listened intently.

Victoria batted her eyelids somewhat shyly. "I was never attracted to him." Her eyes became glassy and distant. "Or his temper."

"What about his temper?"

"He couldn't control it."

"Did he hit you?" Cameron asked softly.

"Yes," she dropped her head and almost immediately started to shed silent tears. "I had to go to the hospital several times. Sometimes he became angry because he thought I was looking at another man."

"He figured that since he paid for you he could treat you however he wanted. Were you seeing anyone?"

"I never cheated on him. In my country we are taught to accept what God has given us." She locked eyes with Cameron again. "My loyalty didn't matter though. I found out that Robert had this private eye friend."

"Do you know the name?"

"Yes. Eddie Zimbardo."

"I know him." Cameron wasn't surprised that Big Eddie was involved with this case. "How was he involved?"

"Robert had Eddie watch me constantly. Day and night this man or one of his men would follow me."

"Did Eddie report anything?" Cameron asked.

"Like I said, there was nothing to report, Lieutenant."

Cameron believed her. His sixth sense told him so. He decided to change topics. "So, tell me, did you know that your husband had a gambling problem?"

"Of course," Victoria seemed to relax again. "But I only heard about it from him when he won."

"Did he win often?"

"No, but his latest bet was a big win. Enough to clear him of his debt." Victoria shook her head in disgust. "He would bet on anything and everything. This time he bet on some woman to win a fight. She apparently was fighting this oriental woman that was supposed to never lose. Robert went for the long shot, like he always did, and finally won one. The oriental woman lost."

Cameron had witnessed that sort of gambling craze many times. He was already feeling drained from this interview and decided now was the time to spring the main question at her. "Tell me, did you hate your husband enough to kill him?"

She laughed. "Of course I hated him enough and I can even say that I wish I were strong enough, but no, Lieutenant, I didn't kill him."

"Where were you on the night that he was put in the hospital?"

"I was here."

"Alone?"

"Yes. Except for the customary stakeout of that private eye."

Cameron left Victoria Lancaster's house with an empty, bewildered, feeling. He drove slowly back to Peachtree Street and, of course, checked from time to time to see if his tag-a-long thugs were nearby. They were. The whole conversation at Victoria Lancaster's house led to complete and utter confusion. Robert Lancaster had a suicide attempt history. But he was the type that wrote a suicide note. There were people who would probably love to get even with him. And then there was Big Eddie. Who knows, maybe Victoria talked Big Eddie into helping her out.

CHAPTER 15

WASHINGTON, D.C.
JUNE 2001

WHILE WAITING for Larry Colburn to show up for a meeting, Triplett decided to put an idea, a straw man, on the table to see if the Catfish would bite. The straw man game plan was simple in Triplett's mind. He would have someone approach Vance Connelly with a deal. Perhaps he would even pay the good doctor a personal visit. Triplett knew of four drugs that were about to be reinvented, so to speak. The industry called it "wintergreening." The chemical compound of the drug isn't significantly changed but by adding or subtracting a chemical buffer, it can be labeled as "new and improved", patented and then marketed as a "name brand" not available in generic form. Anybody with the inside scoop could buy stock and make a fortune. Maybe Connelly would appreciate easy retirement funds.

Senator Adams rebuffed the idea flat out. "I've been down that road before and you're barking up the wrong tree. You can't win by trying to buy Connelly."

Maybe the senator was so forthright because it was late on Friday evening. Maybe the Senator was tired of Triplett. But neither reason was of any concern for Triplett. No, he didn't care where the senator was, emotionally or physically.

Triplett studied the senator's face. He sat silently, waiting for the senator to notice that he was getting increasingly annoyed. For a fleeting moment Triplett thought he should give Henderson a hefty donation for a future senatorial candidacy. In a snap, Senator Adams could be history.

Triplett ran his oversized hands above his ears to slick back his horseshoe-crown of white hair. His stare never wavered from the senator. The senator's bloodshot nose turned redder by the minute.

The senator got the hint and settled down. He blinked and said hesitantly, "At least, I wouldn't recommend that you attempt this game plan."

The senator recalled his last encounter with Connelly in front of the Senate Health Committee hearings. He had tried everything to keep Connelly from testifying, but wasn't able to control him. "That stubborn sonofabitch Connelly can't be blackmailed or bribed."

Triplett mulled over the senator's perspective. A considerable silence passed before he spoke.

"I believe you." Triplett let the soft soap sell slide.

The Catfish stood up and moved to the wet bar. He didn't want Triplett to see how relieved he was that they had agreed. "Care for a cocktail?"

That was like asking somebody in hell if he was hot and thirsty. Triplett nodded. They barely said a word as they consumed their first round.

Soon they were rattling ice cubes and ready for refills. By the time Larry Colburn arrived, they were midway into their second drink. The senator had been planning this meeting for over a week and Colburn was late.

"Sorry, my flight was delayed." Colburn looked haggard.

"You look like something the cat dragged in from a swamp." Senator Adams said, indulging himself with a Mississippi analogy. He poured Colburn a double scotch, neat.

Colburn described his recent activities. His meeting with Quincy. His search around Greystone. The bottom line was that he had discovered nothing worthwhile. Not a single strand for the legal sharks to twist and turn, at least not on Vance Connelly. But Vance had a team. And there was one team member in particular that Colburn thought he could use to cast a disparaging shadow over Vance. That person was Bill Barringer.

NEW YORK, NEW YORK
JUNE 2001

Live, from Studio 33. Every Sunday morning the TV press had a showdown on a major topic confronting America. This week was a hot topic that affected virtually every American. The program would be devoted to the declining state of the health care system. Sitting in a hot studio and facing an opponent who threw hardball questions like E.B. Goodroe, was not Vance's idea of a perfect Sunday morning. Originally, Vice President Lancaster was going to be a guest on the talk show, but he was detained in a Middle East peace meeting. Vance was called at the last minute on Saturday afternoon. He was lucky to catch a late flight to New York and get a few hours of sleep.

The conservative block of the media was targeting President Hillgren's favorite items on his national agenda. He called his plan "The Future Society" and one of his most important goals was revamping the health care system.

E.B. Goodroe's role was to keep order and ask thought provoking questions. Goodroe was an old style newsroom reporter. He attained his fame by doing battlefield reporting during the Vietnam War. He had a rugged, worn face with a scar above his right eye that extended to his hairline. He never talked about the scar, but it was known that he got it defending wounded comrades in a foxhole. Fire popped all around and the one bullet that grazed his head almost ended his career. He was tough from years of experience and was trusted by the American public.

Opposing participants in the debate were announced to be Mr. Ron Triplett and Dr. Vance Connelly. Goodroe spelled out their credentials. He told the audience that Triplett was the CEO of the large drug and medical instrument company, Speck MediSurge, and he also served on the boards of several Health Maintenance Organizations. Goodroe then gave equal importance to Vance's career as a well published cardiologist and as a physician who was a member of the president's health care reform committee.

Prior to going on the air Triplett approached Vance and casually extended his oversized hand. Connelly caught a glimpse of Triplett's gold ring. He felt a brief adrenaline rush. The ring instantly bothered him. Why? His mind raced to place the image. There was something negative about it. He just wasn't sure. They sized each other up and in that moment a strong sense of distrust formed between them.

The air in the studio matched their discomfort. The air was downright stale to Vance. He found it difficult to breathe. It was hot under the lights. Very hot.

The introduction of the topic and the participants was brief. The network had cleverly placed a caduceus, the symbol of medicine, between the participants. The screen was light blue and the caduceus a variety of sharp coordinated golden colors. Lights, camera, action.

"Dr. Connelly, I would like to begin our questions with you." Goodroe pointed to the caduceus. "The ancient symbol of the medical profession, the caduceus, has always stood for the best. Tell me, sir, what's your opinion of the current health care system?"

Vance was expecting that as an opening question. It was designed to relax him. The heat from the lights seemed to drop a degree or two. "Unfortunately, Mr. Goodroe, I'm afraid that the caduceus is currently tarnished. It's deeply imbedded in the health care system that includes the profession of medicine, lawyers, industry, and politics. The unethical behavior of each part of the system has tarnished the profession of medicine."

"A tarnished caduceus?" Goodroe smiled and then slipped in a question designed to give his audience a visual. "Do you mean like rust coating a nail?"

"I'm afraid it's deeper than just a coating. The rust has eaten away some of the nail." Vance was enjoying the way Goodroe led him into a comfortable dialogue. "It is better to be sick today than it was 50 years ago. There are improved medicines, better techniques and advanced technology. Despite the advances, I believe the current system of health care is failing."

"How so?" Goodroe began to quicken the pace. "How can you say that it is better to be sick now than 50 years ago and, at the same time call the current system a failure?"

Vance didn't need to reflect to answer. "Research. Medical research has brought spectacular results. We now have more diagnostic and treatment methods. That's the good part. The bad part is that we are unable to deliver the fruits of research to all the people who need it."

"Why can't we deliver it?" Goodroe asked.

"Because the cost of delivering medical care to every person is currently not possible. And, in addition, good doctors are forced to work in a bad system."

"Mr. Triplett, your thoughts?" Goodroe asked.

"I'm not sure why Dr. Connelly feels that way. Government programs such as Medicare for the elderly and Medicaid, and the private, highly successful, HMO's created by the private sector, were developed specifically for the purpose of delivering affordable health care. And, frankly, I'm surprised that Doctor Connelly would describe health care delivery as being impossible. This is simply a financial reality. Medical care, if given like Dr. Connelly would like to provide, would bankrupt our country."

"Dr. Connelly, according to Mr. Triplett we have programs in place to deliver health care." Goodroe repeated.

Vance hesitated for a second before answering. His mind was momentarily distracted trying to find the meaning of Triplett's ring. He gave the ring another glance and saw it glistening under the bright lights of the studio. It was imprinted in his mind somewhere. He answered Goodroe. "Medicare for the elderly has been somewhat successful because patients can choose their own doctor. But Medicare does not cover all the cost of all the medical services that are needed and does not pay for expensive drugs. Doctors cannot keep their offices open and pay their office staff, when only Medicare patients fill their schedule."

"Of course not," Triplett fired back. "The system isn't designed to be a free ride for physicians. It's designed to help create a balance of resources. Doctors aren't supposed to stop their free enterprise activities altogether."

Vance shook his head. "Some doctors must pay $100,000 for malpractice insurance because lawyers encourage patients to sue doctors for the most frivolous reasons. Surely, anyone can see that is why some doctors can't continue to see patients. If they do continue to see patients they are forced to increase their fees in order to survive."

Connelly continued, "Unfortunately, we have 40 million people who do not have access to any health care program because they don't have health insurance. They can't afford it. These people, when they get sick, can't support the financial aspects of a doctor's office or the high cost of service in an emergency clinic. I think both the public and private sectors are failing. I personally believe this nation can do better."

"Of course they can do better." Triplett replied without missing a beat. "They can do better by learning how to run it as a competitive business. They need to catch up with the corporate world and develop strategies for cost control, competition and intensive marketing."

Vance replied with equal vigor, "A serious by-product of the current system, a system modeled on what Mr. Triplett is advocating, is that it is killing the spirit of practicing doctors. This in turn is causing a deterioration of the medical profession itself. Mr. Triplett must understand that many well qualified college students do not choose medicine as a career because of the chaos currently found in the health care system. Also, applications to nursing schools have decreased to a dangerous level. Without skilled nurses, hospitals can't possibly provide even the most basic care. Nurses are underpaid, under appreciated and harassed."

Goodroe broke into the discussion. "Ok, folks. You can see that we have a great discussion here. And we will continue when we come back after a word from our sponsors." Connelly and Triplett each drank some water and then thoughtfully inspected each other. The network cut away for a commercial break.

After the advertisement of a new and improved natural weight loss product was sandwiched in between two soda commercials, the studio was back to the interview.

Goodroe gave a quick summary of the proceedings and picked up the debate with Triplett. "Dr. Connelly is worried that the number of qualified college students that want to be doctors and nurses is decreasing. What are your thoughts about that, Mr. Triplett?"

"Physicians rank among the highest paid people in the world. I don't think we'll see a mass exodus from the profession anytime soon. Besides, it's basic supply and demand. If we start to lose good physicians I would expect that the system would adjust and provide an increase in physician's income."

"And the nurses?" Goodroe questioned.

"Business always has its ebb and flow." Triplett stuck to his free enterprise concept. "Over time the system will correct itself."

Vance couldn't help the passion in his reply. "You simply don't understand, this isn't about money, it's about spirit! The system, as Mr. Triplett sees it, is destroying the spirit of good doctors and nurses. They are controlled by managed health care systems that are programmed to make money. Please remember, that most young people enter the medical profession because they want to help people. The true professionals of our field do not develop their skills in order to make piles of money. That is not used to measure their success."

"You can talk noble all you like," Triplett retorted quickly, "It is not about some old fashioned attitude, it's about business. Every businessman knows that doctors don't have a clue about business." Triplett cast his eyes directly at Vance. "The goal of any good business is to produce a profit. We all fail when the bottom-line falls short. Period. This is the way the system works. Dr. Connelly can be idealistic all he wants, but if the medical system fails to produce the appropriate financial outcomes then we will all suffer."

Goodroe had given them plenty of rope and decided to step into the debate. "Dr. Connelly, you say there has been a decline in the medical care system. What do you think caused this deterioration?"

Vance turned a sharp look toward Triplett and replied. "People like Mr. Triplett only define health care success in terms of income and profit margins. In my opinion, the profession of medicine and the delivery of care began to spiral downward when the people who seized the financial strings of the profession and proclaimed that they intended to operate the health care delivery system as a business guided by market forces!"

"Now it is you, Dr. Connelly, that simply doesn't understand." Triplett said harshly. "The pressure of market forces is keeping cost down."

Vance didn't flinch at Triplett's attempt to intimidate him. "I'll give a good example of your market force at work. The CEO of an HMO makes millions of dollars a year. His or her annual increase in salary is made possible only by curtailing patient services. This, of course, places a vice on the doctor's freedom to prescribe the best for patient's problems." Vance punctuated his statement, "That is your market forces at work!"

Triplett started to reply but Vance held up his hand and continued talking. "I'll give you another simple example of your market force influence. You pay advertising agencies huge amounts of money to market your drugs. This also increases the cost of medical care. Let me tell you sir, we physicians have learned that the more you market the less the value of the drug!" Then Vance challenged Triplett, "Therefore, I urge you and other CEO's who run pharmaceutical houses to stop advertising in the newspaper and lay magazines."

Triplett half rose out of his chair. His face was flushed. "You can't compete without marketing!"

Vance bristled. "When a real break-through occurs it sells itself almost immediately. When penicillin was discovered there was no need to advertise its value in popular magazines and newspapers."

"That was a different era. An industry wouldn't survive today without an extensive marketing effort. It doesn't harm anyone. It only informs people of the availability of the drugs and new technology."

Vance looked straight at Triplett and said, "You're wrong, Mr. Triplett. It does considerable damage. It creates unrealistic expectations in the minds of patients. They go to a doctor and demand a medicine based on the slick advertising created by the marketing firm. The patient then tries to tell the doctor what they need for treatment whether it is appropriate or not. This causes an erosion of trust in the relationship between the patient and the doctor."

Triplett tossed a different spin. "I believe that the American people are sufficiently intelligent to sort out the facts themselves. By giving them information they have the opportunity to explore alternatives. I would never insult the people of this great country by telling them they shouldn't be exposed to information."

"Information is one thing, advertising is another." Vance wasn't going to let Triplett slide this argument into a different discussion. "Advertising twist information to make an appeal for choosing something. I have seen hospitals forced to advertise. Some will claim they are the best with no information to back up their claim."

There was a pause and the two guests maintained eye contact.

"Mr. Triplett." Goodroe inserted. "So far, you have emphasized the need to approach health care with a business perspective. Could you speak more about this need?"

Triplett was visibly upset. "In the past there were no cost controls on doctors. By bringing in a business mentality, we have been able to start turning the system into viable cost centers. Some HMO's are even on the big board in New York and their stocks are doing well. How can Dr. Connelly possibly ignore the fact that this financial approach has been good for the health care industry? Many investors are quite happy because their stock has done so well. In fact, if we had left things alone there probably would be no health care system at all."

Goodroe quickly turned to Vance. "Any comment on this, Dr. Connelly?"

"Yes." Vance answered. "Mr. Triplett set the stage beautifully for my response. I couldn't help but notice that he only talks about profit and the stock market. In addition to being a CEO for a pharmaceutical house, Mr. Triplett makes a large amount of money serving on the board and having stock in several HMO's. So he is in perfect position to gain from both sources. Each feeding the other."

Triplett didn't respond. Instead he leaned back in his chair and glared at Vance.

Vance continued. "Where does the money come from in those HMO's? It comes from the services rendered by physicians who see patients. I must insist, the delivery of a specialized service, like medicine, is a profession and not a business. I think this is where Triplett and I disagree the most. His definition of a profession is limited in scope. He seems to think that a business, such as an HMO, is a profession because it makes money. I'm here to emphasize that medicine cannot be successful if it is operated solely from a business mindset because such an approach disregards the doctor's dedication to do the best for their patients."

"Mr. Triplett," Goodroe excelled at remaining neutral, "do you feel like you are limiting the scope of medicine by focusing on it as a business?"

"If I am, it is only because it is the business aspect of health care that is the most out of control. Cost control needs to be emphasized until we can truly control the cost. I don't know all the aspects of the medical profession, but I can certainly tell you that every business has to make a profit. No profit, no business. Business professions exist because there are money-making opportunities. Businesses are not charity organizations where goods are given away. Money is the bottom line."

The cameraman motioned for a commercial break.

This time there was a hyped-up purple pill antacid and a Lexus commercial followed by a teasing preview of the weekend's sports events.

During the break Vance caught another glimpse at Triplett's ring. The image suddenly hit him. It seemed to pop in his mind's eye from nowhere. Vance remembered how Cameron had explained the gold ring and its meaning from the Lancaster case of 1952. Vance knew who he was dealing with now. Triplett was a member of the mob.

When they returned to the set, Goodroe opened immediately with a brief review of Triplett's comments followed by a question for Vance.

"Dr. Connelly, how do you respond to Mr. Triplett's viewpoint?"

"Again, I find his views to be narrow and limited. The idea that the medical profession revolves solely around money leaves a lot to be desired."

Goodroe pushed. "What would you add, doctor?"

"That the members of a profession should be the ones who set standards for their performance and that the profession should be self regulating. The activities must not be controlled by people who have no knowledge of the professional service that is delivered."

Triplett tossed in a low blow. "Now, that would put the fox in charge of the hen house, wouldn't it?"

Vance ignored him. "The fact is, the medical profession has a body of knowledge that is understood by its members and not by others. It takes highly trained members of the profession to judge the competence of those who practice the profession. It takes 11 years or more after high school of intensive study to make a doctor. It also cost a great deal of money to do that. It just doesn't make sense for a doctor to have to spend excessive amounts of time validating critical decisions about a patient to a cost watchdog at an HMO who not only has no medical qualifications, but isn't even present where the decisions are made. That sort of system will ultimately erode the trust patients have developed for doctors."

"Why would this erode trust?" Triplett inquired. "Now Dr. Connelly is being short sighted. The present system doesn't erode trust; it does the opposite. Our system builds trust. Trust for the future. Our present system paves the way for us to ensure that there is a medical profession in the future. We have to instill in the minds of doctors that the spiraling cost must be controlled or eventually there will be no hospital doors to open. Like it or not, Dr. Connelly, the business side of health care is like any other business. It is 'red in tooth and claw' and only the fittest will survive."

Goodroe pointed to Vance. "We have time for a short rebuttal, Dr. Connelly."

"I disagree with Mr. Triplett on the trust issue. It goes deeper than he suggests. Patients trust their doctors because doctors performed well over a long period of time. Accordingly, doctors must have a free hand to retain their patient's trust. When administrators and clerks make decisions about the proper treatment of a patient, the doctor's hands are tied and they can't implement the best for the patient. This, Mr. Triplett, is what erodes trust."

"For the most part," Triplett tossed in a jab, "doctors have a monopoly. It's their game to lose when it comes to trust."

"And," Vance held up his hand, "when patients are required to change doctors frequently, a trusting relationship cannot be established. I also disagree with Mr. Triplett's statement that the health care system is like any other business. The practice of medicine is a humanitarian act, and that is where the focus should be."

"You're not thinking about the bottom line again, doctor." Triplett was sitting up straighter, his eyes challenging.

"The bottom line is obvious, Mr. Triplett." Vance replied. "I talk about people and their needs. And, from my point of view, I believe that Oscar Wilde would say that you, Mr. Triplett, know the cost of everything and the value of nothing."

Triplett's jaw clenched. "Doctor, you talk like all those in the medical profession are saints—that they never do any harm to their patients."

Vance inserted quickly. "Thank you for calling me doctor instead of a health care provider. And I also appreciate that you referred to sick people as patients instead of customers."

Triplett paused to take in the twist on words that Vance presented.

"I agree with you, Mr. Triplett," Vance again was catching Triplett off guard. "There are some doctors who don't act professionally although they are in the profession of medicine."

"They cheat Medicare and other systems," Triplett snapped. "Or do shoddy research for pharmaceutical companies, and some doctors are plain incompetent!"

Vance nodded in agreement. "Yes, that's true. And they are ostracized by the watchdogs of the profession and properly sued by lawyers. But let me make myself clear. I want to say this as *strongly* as I can, Mr. Triplett. I recognize that it is the good businesses of this country that make an honest and proper profit that make this country great. The leaders of those great companies have been successful without hurting anyone, commonly giving a great deal of money for hospitals, medical research, universities, parks, art centers and the like. They, sir, are magnificent. This, of course, isn't what I'm talking about. Although I wonder how much you and Speck MediSurge have given back to the system or to the people."

Triplett stuck up his hand. "Before you jump to conclusions, you ought to check out what we have done. You may be surprised."

Vance knew that Triplett would have the customary smoke screen, all properly written out by lawyers and accountants, of contributions back to the system. He decided not to call Triplett's bluff. "I am simply stating, sir," Vance was determined not to be pulled off track, *"that no one should make an unreasonable profit from sick people and that the profession of medicine must deliver the best of care to all who need it whether or not they can afford it."*

Triplett wasn't prepared for Vance to shift gears. The cat had his claws. Only the glare of his eyes would leave a lasting impression on the television camera.

Vance finished. "No one should be proud of an HMO that is on the big board because, in order to be listed there, it is necessary to withhold medical services from the sick people it claims to serve."

The background music for the E.B. Goodroe News Hour began to play. The lights faded and the dark silhouettes of the participants remained fixed while the credits rolled.

Their time was finished. The hour had gone too quickly for this Sunday morning talk show.

Once they were officially off the air, Goodroe shook hands with each of them and thanked them for participating. Triplett and Vance didn't shake hands or even speak as they departed.

Vance thought that he stated his case fairly well. Of course, he had already thought of a dozen things he wished he had said. But more importantly he wanted to get a tape of this interview from Goodroe. He wanted some experts to zoom in on Triplett's ring in order to see the mob emblem more clearly.

———◆———

Senator Adams was still laughing when he hit the remote and turned off the TV. "I told Triplett that he was dealing with a smart son-of-a-bitch. He knows it now, Neil Henry."

Neil had his own smile. He hated Triplett with an ever-growing passion. He was also hoping that Pamela saw the show today. In the midst of his hopes the phone rang.

The senator sounded delighted. "Hello Pamela! Did you see the big talk show?" The senator flipped their conversation to the speakerphone.

"Yes." Pamela sounded in high spirits. She had gotten to know Vance, now that she was working with him, and she had to admit that the old doctor had gained her respect. Besides, Pamela was tired of playing Triplett's games.

"What else did you do on this fine Sunday besides sit around and watch a health debate?" Senator Adams asked.

"Believe it or not I went to church." Pamela replied. She had stepped into the Methodist church where her brother, Josh, preached. She'd taken a seat in the back where Josh wouldn't notice her and made a quick exit during the final hymn. She didn't really know what made her go to see him. She had long ago quit believing in God and she had long ago quit getting in touch with her family. But something seemed to guide her there. Something made her listen today.

The senator was taken back. "Girl, this sure is a damn drastic change in your character."

Pamela figured that she would take a few wise cracks from the senator, but she was drawn to go see her brother and she was glad she did.

The senator stood up and strolled over to the bar. He put two ice cubes in a glass and then topped it with 25 year old MaCallan. "And what did the preacher man say?"

Pamela didn't want to beat around the bush. "I take it Larry Colburn talked to you recently? Did he tell you that Triplett told him to get in touch with me?"

"Yes. The information you gave him was genius, my dear." The senator took a sip of his single malt. "How did you pull that off?"

"Once I set up the computer system, I was able to put a Trojan horse into Connelly's and Barringer's files. If you really know computers you can retrieve anything."

"You were able to retrieve files that contained private medical records?" Neil Henry asked.

Pamela knew Neil would appreciate her skills.

"To make a long story short," Pamela opened the refrigerator while she talked. She pulled out some cold pizza and a beer and closed the refrigerator door with a swing of her hip. "The patient described in the file is a long time friend of Barringer's. He is a severe diabetic who smokes and drinks a lot and has been unhealthy for years. Barringer apparently knew that and during a check-up, discovered that his friend's heart was in really bad shape."

"How did you know this guy is a friend of Barringer?" the senator asked.

"He works on Barringer's ranch. His name is Jake something or other." Pamela tried to recall. "Anyway, Jake needs a new heart and Barringer is going to bump everybody in line waiting for a donor so his friend can have the next heart transplant."

"Give me the timeline on this." Neil demanded.

"The final diagnosis came in about four days ago. They are moving really fast. Jake enters the hospital tomorrow." Pamela thumbed through her notes. "What makes this important from Larry Colburn's point of view is that Barringer has bumped a mother of four to help his friend."

"Whoa," the senator smiled. "I believe that could lead to a hefty lawsuit, and at the same time, also take down that righteous attitude of his boss, Vance Connelly, a notch or two."

"I want the details, Pamela. And I don't want you to e-mail the stuff. I want it hand delivered." The senator looked at Neil Henry. "I'm sending Neil down on the next flight to get those records."

CHAPTER 16

CHARLESTON, SOUTH CAROLINA
OCTOBER 1952

AFTER VANCE left Robert Lancaster's office, he made a beeline for the airport. He had just enough time to call his secretary and have her reschedule his patients. Luckily his patient load was not very demanding that day.

As soon as his plane landed in Charleston, Vance went to a phone booth. He needed the street address of The Sand Dune condominiums. It was located on the oceanfront.

Traffic in Charleston was rarely thick and the cab driver had a heavy foot. Soon his taxi arrived at an elegant looking structure with impressive landscaping.

He maintained a calm pace as he entered the lobby, observed his surroundings and decided to sit on a couch that was within earshot of the front desk. Vance watched, listened and observed the staff as they helped people with their needs and wishes. It didn't take long for him to figure out that the biggest wheeler-dealer on the staff was at the concierge's desk. The young man knew the names of all the regulars and they, in turn, kept his wallet full.

Vance waited until the young man was alone.

"Excuse me." Vance straightened his tie as he talked. "I'm looking for Robert Lancaster. He was supposed to meet me in the lobby."

"Mr. Lancaster is an owner, isn't he?" The young man replied.

"Yes." Vance stopped tugging his tie. He took his time buttoning his coat and then looked into the young man's eyes. "So, you know who I'm talking about?"

"Of course."

Vance stepped closer. "Do you know if he's here?"

"I'm not supposed to provide that information, sir. I can connect you with his room."

"No, thank you. I'm certain that you can help." Vance pulled out his money clip and handed the young man a twenty.

Tucking the bill in his pocket, the concierge slipped around the desk and checked the reservation book. "He usually calls when he arrives." The young man's face twisted into a puzzled knot. "We have no message from him, sir."

"He was coming from London and he didn't have time to call." Vance looked away from the young man as he talked. "Yes, I'm certain he was coming today."

"Wait a minute," the young man bent down and read a footnote in the book.

Vance leaned forward hoping, praying that it wasn't a note about Robert Lancaster's death. "What?"

"Apparently, an authorized person is occupying his room this week."

Vance dug into his pocket to pull out another $20 and handed it to the young man. "I'm certain that the person occupying the room is who Lancaster wants me to meet. I'd appreciate it if you would tell me the room number and let me find my own way."

The young man again stuffed the bill into his pocket. "You're really asking me to risk my job, sir."

Vance handed him another $20, "Like I said, I want the room number."

This time he didn't hesitate. "Room 455."

"And the master key?"

"Are you crazy?"

Vance leaned closer. "What's it worth?"

"At least a C note."

Vance frowned.

"Ok, I'll do it for 50." The young man was nervous. "I'm going to put the key on the desk and then I'm going to walk away."

Vance nodded and slipped him the 50 bucks.

The young man looked casually around and then opened the desk drawer. He pulled out the master key and placed it on top of the desk, then quickly strolled to the main door to serve another customer.

Vance took the key and headed to the lounge. From there he dialed Room 455. No answer. He waited 10 minutes and tried again. No answer. He decided to make his move. His heart pounded as the elevator climbed to the fourth floor. His breathing quickened as he approached the room. Vance tried to steady himself as he nervously put the key into the lock. At first the key didn't turn. He jiggled the key harder. Click. The door opened. The lights were off. Vance entered and let his eyes adjust.

He thought about turning around. His guts were telling him to run. But he fought the impulse. Flipping on the light, he advanced into the room. It was a two bedroom condo. The first bedroom was on the left. The kitchen and den were combined into a great room. The master bedroom was beyond the kitchen and the balcony was attached to the den.

The guest bedroom was undisturbed. No sign of anyone. The refrigerator was stocked with a few selected items. OJ. Milk. Fruit. Cold cuts. Two bottles of wine. The master bedroom had been straightened. The clothes in the closet let Vance know that a female was staying there. The condo was much larger than he had anticipated. Lancaster obviously spent a great deal of time here. He had small personal items everywhere.

Vance found a stack of letters in the nightstand drawer. They were signed, "Love always." He read one of them. The person who wrote it was desperate for Lancaster to hurry and leave his wife. She couldn't wait to be in his arms forever. The oldest letter was dated 1950. Their affair was not a flash in the pan. It had lasted for more than two years.

Vance stopped reading and looked around for more clues, searching the bedroom and den. Nothing of real importance. He walked to the balcony. He remembered the picture of Jennifer smiling. He flipped on the balcony light.

There sitting in a chair with a glass of wine, was Jennifer Eden. She was slouched with her feet up on the edge of the railing. Her stare as cold as ice.

"I saw you enter." She took a sip of wine and maintained her stare. "Did you find what you're looking for?"

Vance was speechless. He had thought that he was alone, but instead Jennifer had been watching.

"I said," she spoke harshly, "did you find what you're looking for?"

"I'm still looking."

Jennifer's face looked tired and pale. She wore no make-up and her clothes were wrinkled. Her hair was brushed back away from her face. Despite all of that she was still beautiful. "So, now you *think* you know my little secret."

Vance leaned on the railing and looked out over the city. The lights were bright and the night air was cool. "I'd rather you spell it out."

"First you tell me. What do you think is happening?"

Vance still felt a strange pull towards Jennifer. He knew he was attracted to her but there was something else. A deeper feeling. A feeling that they had known each other for ages. "I think," Vance broke out of his spell and turned toward her, "that you were having an affair with Robert Lancaster."

Jennifer smiled. "Close, but not quite right."

Vance paused, waiting for her to tell him her story.

"My sister was having the affair."

Vance was taken by surprise. He thought he had figured it all out. "I saw a picture of you here."

"I joined them here for a long weekend once." Jennifer sipped her wine.

"Then why are you up here now instead of her?"

Jennifer didn't answer. She shuffled her body and took another sip of wine.

Vance cleared his throat. "Did she do it?"

Jennifer's eyes started to tear. "No. She could never hurt him. She loved him."

"She's been coming up here for some time, hasn't she?"

"Actually, they met several years ago, but it started off as a friendship. I don't think Brooke ever intended to have their relationship evolve like it did."

"How did they meet?"

"She worked in Dr. Wasserman's office as a secretary."

"So she met Robert when he became Harold's patient."

She didn't answer, instead choosing to pull at the blanket on her legs.

"Did she know he was married?"

"She knew that he was unhappily married."

"And somehow she fell in love with him?"

Jennifer cocked her head defensively. "Brooke didn't just see him and start running around with him, if that's what you think."

"No." Vance was more careful in his choice of words. "I'm sure she had her reasons."

Vance felt the bond Jennifer had for her sister.

Jennifer couldn't seem to get comfortable with the blanket. She pulled it tighter to her waist. "Robert told her he was going to leave his wife."

"And she believed him?"

"Absolutely." She explained. "He was just waiting for his wife to make a mistake. Robert didn't want the courts to bleed him dry over a divorce."

"He was rich?" Vance asked knowingly.

"Yes, but that had nothing to do with Brooke's love for him."

It looked to Vance as though Jennifer and Brooke knew nothing about the real Robert Lancaster. To them he was a good man with a kind heart. And, of course, he was going to leave his awful wife and marry Brooke.

"Jennifer, you have to come back and talk to the police."

"I know, but I've been afraid that they might think Brooke had something to do with his death."

"Why?"

"You know the picture of the jealous girlfriend stuff that they would try to paint."

Vance stood up. "It will look worse if Brooke doesn't meet with them."

Jennifer pushed off her blanket and walked into the condo. She took a sweeping look at the room. She felt comfortable with Vance and wanted to trust him. She wasn't sure because many days had been filled with fear and worry. She knew what she was doing wasn't working. It was time to face reality. It was time to have Brooke clear herself.

Jennifer got her things together and Vance called for airline reservations. They were scheduled for a late night flight back to Atlanta.

CHAPTER 17

WASHINGTON, D.C.
JULY 2001

EVERYONE WAS preparing for the Fourth of July. Parades and speeches would take over the Nation. President Hillgren was putting the finishing touches on his soon to be televised speech. His speechwriters provided a spirited patriotic discourse designed to paint everything rose-colored and on track in the greatest country on earth. Nothing controversial. Nothing new. Just rhythm and emotion. Something easy and palatable to say while the American people enjoyed eating barbecue and taking in displays of fireworks that ranged from backyard bottle rockets and sparklers to extraordinary public extravaganzas set to music.

Hilgren wasn't pleased with the speech. He wanted this Fourth of July to be a springboard for pushing his agenda forward. He wanted something with real teeth in it. He didn't agree with those who advised against giving a hardball political speech.

President Hillgren listened but stood fast in his desire to act as a leader and not a cheerleader. He invited Vance and Bill to the White House to help him with the medical part of the speech. Sometimes a

President has to rock the boat a bit to get the citizens fired up and motivated.

The President was standing by the window in the Oval Office when Vance and Bill entered. The President's secretary had learned long ago not to disrupt him when he was in a reflective mood. She quietly ushered Vance and Bill in and had them sit on a couch. They sat there motionless and looked at the silhouette of the President standing with folded arms.

All was quiet in the Oval Office for some time before the President began to speak.

"Gentlemen, over the last two days my advisors have been telling me to lay low. That the polls show that I'm a popular president at the moment. They tell me that I don't need to do anything to cause controversy or upset the apple cart."

The President turned and looked at his guests. "Do you know what I think of that kind of strategy?"

Vance and Bill knew that the President wasn't really looking for them to speak so they remained silent.

"Well, gentlemen," the President walked over and stood before them. "The type of lay low strategy that is designed to fight fires only when they pop up is a coward's way of running the country." The President shook his head, "We can stick our heads in the sand and pretend everything is fine but we all know in reality we have to do something and we have to do it now. We must change our outdated systems of education, health and welfare. And most important— we need to redefine what we stand for as a country. It's time to spend my political capital to help this country."

Vance and Bill were taken aback by the President's candid comments. They were honored that the President had trusted them to vent his frustrations. They made no response; it was a time to listen.

"A few weeks ago I was in England. I started thinking then that I wanted to use the Fourth of July to highlight my agenda. I want controversy. I want action."

The President gave Vance and Bill a brief handshake before he sat down. "Now this is what I want from you." The President looked at Vance momentarily with a blank stare. It wasn't long, yet it was an awkward moment. A sudden struggle of consciousness. Seconds later an expression of relief came over the President's face as he continued. "Vance." For a flashing moment the President had misplaced Vance's name. "I want to push up the time frame on the white paper that the health commission is putting together. I want to announce that you'll complete your subcommittee part of the report in three months rather than a year. I've reviewed what you have done so far and I want you to go faster."

"Mr. President," Vance was caught off guard. His timetable was laid out and schedules were made. "Of course, we'll give it a shot, but..."

The President clapped his hands as if it were settled. "Good, that's all I can expect." He stood up and walked over to his desk. "Now, gentlemen, I want you to hear how I've positioned the health care issue in my talk tomorrow night."

Vance and Bill spent the rest of the afternoon with the President helping him with his speech. His speech carried the tone of an impatient man with a strong sense of urgency. The speech certainly had the potential of overshadowing the fireworks of the evening. The President wanted his own strategy. A strategy designed to leave no stone unturned.

———◆———

Pamela was on the computer when Neil Henry knocked on the door of her apartment. She had expected him to arrive several hours earlier. His flight was late again. He was coming down for his scheduled weekend. She yelled for him to come on in as she finished pulling together more documents for Vance. Actually, she found the work interesting. She pulled an article from a computer search engine. The article stated that doctors spent as much time seeing patients as they ever did, but the quality of the time spent was less satisfying to the doctors and patients.

She closed her file and stood up to meet Neil Henry.

"Neil!" Pamela walked over to him and gave him a hug. He barely responded.

Neil Henry stuffed his hands into his pockets and half smiled as she backed away from him. He stood still, awkwardly jiggling the coins in his pocket. He looked different for some reason.

Pamela wondered what was up as she led him toward the kitchen to pull out a bottle of Silver Oak chardonnay from her refrigerator. He was silent as she poured the wine. Handing him his glass, she waited for his news.

"There is something I've been meaning to tell you for a long time, Pamela."

Neil took a sip of wine. "It's about Bill Barringer."

"What about him?"

"Remember a few years ago when we were trying to control Vance Connelly's testimony to the Senate?"

She nodded.

Neil cleared his throat. "Did you ever wonder why we couldn't control Connelly?"

Pamela looked hard into Neil Henry's face. "What are you trying to say, Neil?"

"I'm gonna tell you something that I haven't told anyone else." Neil took several sips of wine. He didn't really care if it tasted good or bad. He wanted something to take the edge off. Something. "I brought up Bill Barringer because I wanted you to know that I have known Bill for a long time."

Pamela struggled to put the pieces together.

"Bill and I grew up together. He was my neighbor and friend." Neil Henry explained the story of his youth with Bill. How they went to the same schools, played ball together. They grew up together in Mississippi.

Pamela rubbed her forearms. Still in disbelief she replied, "You gave Barringer information that hurt the Senator?"

Neil nodded. "Not only that, I helped Bill make a tape of the senator detailing some of the bribes that were given to the FDA to keep everything the way Speck MediSurge wanted it. That's why we haven't dealt with Barringer and Connelly as the Senator wanted."

Pamela raked her hand through her newly styled platinum blonde hair.

Her green eyes flared. "If the senator finds out you will be killed."

"Yes, I know." Neil walked up to her and put his hands on her shoulders. "I wanted to tell you this because I want to get out of this mess. I want to go away. And," Neil looked deep into her eyes, "I want you to come with me."

Pamela still had that glare in her eyes. "And what makes you think that I will go with you? Why wouldn't I turn you over to the senator?" Suddenly, Pamela's mouth dropped open. "I get it. You must have some angle on me. If I don't go you're planning on doing something that will ruin me, right?"

"Actually, no."

"What's your angle, then?"

"There's not one." Neil confessed. "This is where I find out what I need to know."

"Find out what?"

"If you care for me." Neil knew that the word love would be too strong.

Pamela searched Neil's eyes. He was serious. He loved her so much that he would risk everything.

Pamela broke away from Neil and stood up. She picked up a pack of cigarettes, pulled one out and lit it. She inhaled deeply

The phone rang before Pamela could think of what to say to Neil.

She casually picked up the phone. It was Triplett's secretary with her usual condescending tone. "Pamela?"

"Yes?"

"Mr. Triplett wants to drop by and take you for a short ride."

Pamela was silent.

"Hello?" Mr. Triplett's secretary interjected impatiently.

Pamela turned and saw Neil Henry sitting on the couch. "Tell him... tell him, no."

"My dear," Mr. Triplett's secretary continued, "if it's money you want for your service, I'm certain that Mr. Triplett would be more than happy to give you five or ten dollars."

Pamela replied coolly, "Just tell him I'm bored. I have other plans."

"Now wait a minute." Mr. Triplett's secretary was not amused.

"What's the matter, honey?" Pamela questioned. "Can't you deliver the bad news?"

"I can deliver the message."

"Good." Pamela was enjoying this moment. She felt an almost overwhelming sense of freedom.

Mr. Triplett's secretary gloated. "I'll tell him."

Pamela studied Neil as she hung up the phone. She casually took the last drag of her cigarette and then rubbed it out in an ashtray.

Neil remained silent.

Pamela looked at Neil and said, "You know the information I'm feeding the senator about Barringer?"

"Yes."

"I've been holding out on him." Pamela smiled knowing that Neil was like her. "I've only been giving him half truths."

Pamela looked at her watch. "I'll explain what I've done later but right now I want to go for a walk."

ATLANTA, GEORGIA
JULY 2001

Quincy hurried as he cut across the back of Greystone Hospital. He wanted to be early to his next meeting with Vance. Ten minutes at least. He came to a screeching halt when he saw his friend M Kool Daddy talking to Colburn.

Whatever Colburn was doing, Quincy knew he was up to no good. He waited patiently as he watched Colburn talking to a few employees who were taking a cigarette break. Kool Daddy was in the group. As soon as Colburn walked away Quincy flagged his old friend and watched as Colburn disappeared around the corner of the building.

Quincy nodded at his friend. "He's after something."

Kool Daddy nodded. "No doubt about that."

"Any clue?"

"From what I hear he's diggin' hard into a Dr. Barringer."

"Barringer?"

"Yeah, don't ask me why. He didn't say."

Quincy made a fist and tapped knuckles with his friend before continuing on his way. Deciding to find Colburn and deal with him in his own way, he looped around the back of the building to search for his adversary.

Quincy stopped when he finally caught sight of him. He watched as Colburn interviewed more people, and then he tracked him to a back stairwell of the parking lot. Quincy closed the gap. His heart pounded as he approached Colburn trotting up the stairwell. The door opened and slowly closed on the second floor. Quincy hurried his step. He started to pry the door open when he was slammed hard into the wall. He felt his nose flatten against the concrete and the warmth of his blood. He had not been hit in the face that hard since playing high school baseball when a line drive rocketed into his jaw. He saw stars then and was seeing even more stars now.

"What are you doing following me?"

Quincy recognized the voice. "Well, fancy meeting you here Mr. Colburn."

Colburn grabbed Quincy's collar and spun him around, putting his forearm into Quincy's throat. "I said, why are you following me?"

With his throat half shut off and his nose bleeding profusely, Quincy could barely breathe. The taste of blood made him gag. "Because…" Quincy gurgled blood as he talked, "because I want to know who you are working for and why are you going after Barringer."

Colburn maintained the pressure on Quincy's throat. "It's way out of your league, man."

Quincy was starting to lose consciousness. He felt himself going limp just as Colburn released him. "Now, get your ass outta here."

"No." Quincy gasped for air. "What is it you want?"

"Let me put it to you this way." Colburn pulled Quincy up within a fraction of an inch of his face. "You know that health committee that you're diggin'?"

"What about it?"

"Resign Quincy." Colburn hissed as he opened the door to the second level and pushed Quincy through it. Quincy landed on the floor with a hard thud. "Resign or ruin your damn career."

The door shut slowly and Quincy heard the footsteps disappear down the stairwell. It took 20 minutes to regain his composure with ten of those minutes in the nearest bathroom stopping his nose from bleeding and washing the blood from his body and clothes. The stars that were swirling in his head were all gone, but Colburn's advice to resign was definitely still there.

CHAPTER 18

ATLANTA, GEORGIA
OCTOBER 1952

CAMERON MET Vance on the steps of the hospital. It was a cool morning and Cameron sucked down a cigarette before entering the hospital.

"You better stop that while you can." Vance said without breaking his pace.

Cameron took another quick draw and then tossed it on the sidewalk, stepping on it without breaking stride. "Plan to stop after this pack."

Vance got into the elevator and raked his fingers through his hair. "Have a surprise for you today."

"Nothing surprises me anymore, Doctor."

"I went to Charleston and found Jennifer Eden."

In spite of himself, Cameron showed a hint of surprise in his face. "How did you figure she was in Charleston?"

Other people joined them on the elevator cutting their conversation short. Once they were in Vance's office Cameron heard the quick run down of events. The next hour was spent debating suspect alternatives.

A steady rain covered the streets just in time for rush hour. Traffic was choked across town. While others experienced the stress of the city, Victoria Lancaster sat comfortably in a large tub of hot water that overlooked the very private backyard of the Lancaster house. She loved to lounge while drinking a glass of wine with a bubble bath foaming in the tub. She was looking for her cigarette lighter when she heard a loud noise in the main part of the house. She froze for a second and before she could reach for her towel a man soundlessly appeared in front of her. He wore a dark blue suit and a big smile. His black hair was long and slicked back into a tight ponytail. He said nothing. He just stood there with a vacuous look in his face.

A short man and an Oriental woman appeared beside him. Victoria pulled the rapidly disappearing bubbles in the tub around her. "Who are you? What do you want?" She was close to panic and struggled as her mind froze, making it impossible to determine options. Her composure started to crumble.

"My, my. Aren't you going to invite us into your lovely home, Mrs. Lancaster?" The short man sat a chair a few feet away. "Or should I say, my home?"

Victoria watched as her tormentor pulled out an oversized cigar. "Who the hell are you?"

The minion in the dark blue suit quickly produced a lighter for his boss, an act he had clearly practiced many times. After taking a few quick puffs and admiring his cigar, the seated man answered. "My name is James Evian."

"Well, whoever you are, get the hell out of my house."

Evian laughed and then waived to the Oriental woman.

Within seconds she had Victoria by the roots of her hair, forcing her body to slip over the side of the tub and land with a slap on the tile floor. Pulling Victoria's long, wet leash of hair she made the whimpering woman crawl to the feet of Evian.

"My, my, what a lovely body you have my dear." Evian flicked the ashes of his cigar onto Victoria's chilled skin.

Victoria's head was pulled high, her face contorted with pain. The woman put her foot into Victoria's lower spine and pressed down hard.

"That's enough, Butterfly. I think she gets the point."

Butterfly let loose of her new plaything.

"You see, Mrs. Lancaster, your husband Robert owed me a great deal of money." Evian continued smoking his cigar as he talked down to Victoria blowing the smoke into her face. "As collateral he signed over this little house."

Victoria began to tremble.

"But, your husband died before my lawyers had a chance to check out everything." Evian blew a cloud of smoke into her face. "It appears that your husband thought he was a clever man."

Victoria crossed her arms over her bare chest.

Evian continued. "You know that the paper he signed was worthless. The house is in your name. He couldn't sign it over."

Victoria remained silent.

Butterfly gave Victoria a swift kick in the side.

Holding up his hand, Evian signaled for Butterfly to stop. "Now, now Butterfly, don't be so impatient."

Leaning down into Victoria's pain ridden face, Evian spoke slowly. "There's no need to mar the beauty of this lovely creature. After all, she's going to get the legal papers to this house and sign it over." Evian put his saliva soaked end of the cigar into her mouth and clamped it shut. "Here dear, you should always smoke a cigar when you close a deal."

As abruptly as they had entered, Evian and his friends departed. Victoria spit the cigar out of her mouth. Choking from the smoke and shaking with fear, she slowly got to her feet and wrapped a towel around her. Her rib cage felt as if someone had hit her with a baseball bat. She was sore and sick from the pain. Her first thought was to call the police, but she knew that Evian would only seek revenge if she did.

Slowly, painfully, she made her way up the stairs to her bedroom.

Sitting carefully on the edge of her bed, she picked up the phone and called the police station. She asked for Lieutenant Lee.

Within the hour Cameron and Vance were at her home and Victoria explained what happened.

Her anger and tears would swell and then subside, like crashing waves. She replayed the intrusion into her home. She saw the face of Evian laughing at her and blowing cigar smoke into her face. She recalled with detail how Butterfly humiliated her by forcing her out of the tub and making her crawl like a dog to Evian's feet. The swift kick to her side still throbbed with sharp pain. And now she stood to lose the house.

Cameron and Vance did what they could to comfort Victoria. It was a difficult situation for her. Cameron had a police officer posted by the driveway. Victoria called a friend to stay with her for the night. There was nothing more they could do for now.

CHAPTER 19

LAWRENCEVILLE, GEORGIA.
AUGUST 2001

AS SOON as Bill glimpsed the front door of his ranch house a warm feeling rushed through his body. He felt complete pleasure. At first he wasn't a hundred percent sold on the idea of Connie resigning from her partnership of physicians and staying home. He was worried that she would become restless and bored. After all, she had spent most of her daylight hours with patients and coworkers. Then, like a hot knife slicing through butter, she was out. Years of work outside the home came to an abrupt halt. Bill watched carefully to see how she was going to adjust to her new lifestyle.

Her focus on John helped. The boy seemed happier. Jake appreciated the extra care since he was sick most of the time. He was frail and bug-eyed and constantly short of breath. If Connie didn't feed him, he probably would have just wasted away.

Bill walked into the house around 8 p.m. and put down his briefcase.

He heard Connie talking with Jake in the kitchen. The spicy warm smell of chili permeated the house. Jake was having a beer with his chili.

Connie was stirring the pot and had her back to Bill. Apparently they didn't hear him enter the house.

Jake was giving her advice. "Ya need more heat in this batch. This should be labeled as baby food for Christ's sake."

"Jake, I know you like enough Tabasco to melt the pot but Bill and I are wimps."

"That's why God created beer." Jake took a sip. "Now, please pass me the hottest pepper you've got."

When Connie spun around to hand Jake his pepper she saw Bill and gave him a warm welcoming smile.

Bill sat down across the kitchen table from Jake and watched him take a few bites. Recently Bill moved Jake to the ranch house and gave him the guest bedroom. He was too worried about his health to leave him in his old room adjacent to the barn. Jake was moving slower with each day.

During Jake's last examination, Bill made a diagnosis of dilated cardiomyopathy and heart failure caused by years of excessive alcohol intake and severe diabetes. Jake often joked about the number of pills that Bill had him take. He said that Bill was a "horse doctor." He probably had coronary artery disease too, but Bill knew that diabetics don't always sense the pain of angina or heart attacks.

Watching Jake finish his beer, Bill brought up the idea of an operation. "I told you that I'm thinking about a big procedure to help you."

"Don't wanna try nothing new," Jake replied.

"Listen Jake, there's a procedure that can help you." Even as he spoke Bill reflected on the many lessons his mentor, Vance, had given him. Echoing through Bill's mind was the constant mantra to "never let emotions interfere with clear thinking". So yes, he knew better, but this was Jake. He had to help him, but at the same time, he knew the procedure was too complicated.

"I don't want to say it again," Jake looked strongly at Bill. "I don't want no high and mighty procedure."

"At least think about it, Jake." Connie spoke up. "You may have a lot of years left."

"For what?" Jake half laughed. "To drink another beer or smoke a cigarette or fall asleep on the porch?"

Bill shook his head in denial. "This isn't like you Jake. You're a fighter. You're…"

Jake held his hand up high. "And *you* don't know when to let go."

The words stung Bill like a bee. Jake was his friend for many years. His foreman. His surrogate father.

"Let me go." Jake looked hard into Bill's eyes. "There is life and then there is living."

Connie held back her tears as she listened.

"I love living. You know that Bill." Jake spoke from his heart. "But simply existing ain't living. And I don't wanna be no experiment. I've never dunna a dignified thing in my life." He never let his tired eyes drift from Bill. "At least let me try to die with dignity." Jake paused for a moment. "Don't expect you to understand, Bill. I just expect you to honor it."

Bill felt a lump in his throat the size of an apple. He had seen death many times in his career, yet, to be so close to his heart this time made the pain swell up inside. His eyes watered. He stood up slowly and walked behind Jake. Jake simply sat in his place. He didn't turn. He didn't move as Bill put a hand on his shoulder.

CHARLOTTE, NORTH CAROLINA

Late on a Thursday afternoon in Charlotte was the unofficial start of another crazy crime fighting weekend. The detective had already done enough paperwork for this shift; it was time to hit the streets. He finished filing his reports and had one more administrative task. The homeless guy arrested for selling beer to minors was getting out of jail. The detective looked through the homeless man's belongings. Hardly anything.

Dread-Mon was soon standing in front of the detective. He was shaved, washed and had a haircut. He was looking healthier.

They went through the usual administrative work and then the detective put Dread-Mon's personal items on his desk.

That's when the call came. There had been a robbery in a local bar downtown and the detective was being called in on the case. During the few moments of havoc, Dread-Mon sat quietly. The detective's desk was definitely cramped for space. Dread-Mon looked around the room and focused on an the filing drawer. His eyes widened. There it was just sitting there, the small CD case.

The detective was shouting out orders to everyone. He turned to a street cop and told him to drive Dread-Mon to the edge of the city and let him go. The detective stalked out in a hurry.

The street cop was a bit more sympathetic than the detective and asked Dread-Mon if wanted some coffee for the ride. Dread-Mon thanked him.

As soon the cop turned his back Dread-Mon casually leaned forward and picked up the CD case. He couldn't believe he was doing this. If he got caught he would be thrown back into jail again. His heart pounded as he slipped the case into his shirt. When the cop came back, Dread-Mon was slowly gathering his personal items from the top of the desk.

ATLANTA, GEORGIA

When Dread-Mon hit the outskirts of Atlanta he felt like he had reached the end of his search for the Holy Grail. The ride from North Carolina had been the easiest part of his trip. Maybe the fact that he was clean made the difference. The first trucker who stopped took him all the way to Atlanta. Dread-Mon spent his first night of freedom under a bridge in a small park.

It was noon Friday before Dread-Mon made his way to Greystone Hospital. He snooped around for Barringer. To his delight Barringer was easy to find. Dread-Mon spent several hours secretly watching him.

When Dread-Mon thought the time was right he quickly approached Barringer. As he passed him on the steps outside one of the buildings Dread-Mon whispered the name written on the inside of the CD case, Chris Miller. The name froze Bill in his footsteps. He hadn't heard from Chris in ages. The last time was at a college reunion. He turned and immediately questioned Dread-Mon about his friend.

Dread-Mon told Bill what happened to Miller. "He gave me something to give you." Dread-Mon held the CD case up for Bill to see.

Bill reached out for the case.

"No, you don't understand Doctor." Dread-Mon rubbed his hand across his chin. "Miller promised that you would pay me. He said you'd pay me a bundle."

Bill's mind was spinning. "I don't know what it's worth."

"If some people were chasing him like that, I would figure it's worth about 5 G's."

Bill remained silent. He thought about the type of research Chris performed. It must be something important, something that would make him risk his life.

Dread-Mon pushed harder. "Listen, your friend Miller lost his life off this thing. It's got to be worth a hell of a lot more than what I'm asking."

"I'm not about to hand you $5,000." Bill shook his head. "How do I know those disk haven't been ruined?"

Dread-Mon smiled, showing his chipped yellowish teeth. Fine, he'd walk away.

"Here's the deal." Bill said. "Take it or leave it. I'll get the money but you stay with me until we know the disks are fine. When I see they're good you get the cash."

Dread-Mon wasn't sure about this arrangement. What if Barringer double-crossed him and had the cops there? He didn't want anymore jail time. In spite of himself he asked, "Where do we meet?"

Bill looked at his watch to figure out how long he needed to get to the bank and back. "My office in about two hours."

Dread-Mon rubbed his chin again and said. "I'll be waiting."

The deal went smoothly. Bill had the money, all hundred dollar bills, wrapped up neatly. Dread-Mon didn't even want to count it. He knew where Barringer was and he could always circle back if necessary.

As soon as Bill loaded the first CD and saw it was in fine shape, Dread-Mon bolted out the door. Barringer didn't move a muscle. Instead he stayed on the computer reading the stolen files.

CHAPTER 20

NEW YORK, NEW YORK
AUGUST 2001

TRIPLETT LEANED back in his fine leather chair and waited for Ruth to attend an emergency meeting with him. He knew that her nickname, Ruthless, was given to her by her peers. He liked that. He had always prided himself for being her mentor. Unfortunately, she had permitted a serious problem to develop at Speck MediSurge. A problem that she could have controlled. Mr. Triplett was unhappy with her performance. This was not going to be a pleasant meeting.

Ruth tapped lightly on his door and then entered meekly. She knew it was time to relinquish her hard-nosed bitch role and to demonstrate loyalty to her boss. She realized that she had been summoned to Mr. Triplett's office to answer to him and she had better look as if she were sorry.

Mr. Triplett pointed to a chair across from him. His secretary brought a fresh cup of coffee and placed it carefully on the desk in front of him. He didn't ask her to pour a cup for Ruth.

Ruth waited patiently while Triplett took a few sips of coffee.

He smiled and leaned forward. "I want an update on our A-42 project."

Ruth felt her throat constrict. It was hard to swallow. "Well sir…"

"Ruth, I've heard rumors. Bad rumors." Mr. Triplett enjoyed making her squirm, "I've heard that things have gotten out of control. Rumors which," he flashed an unsympathetic look at her, "should have been managed before they even had a chance to take seed, let alone spread like a crop of weeds."

Ruth's throat tightened another notch. She looked like her collar was two sizes too small.

"Just give me the facts, Ruth. What are we dealing with here?"

Ruth opened her brief case and slid a few papers across the desk. "Well sir, as you can see the A-42 project has a few roadblocks."

Mr. Triplett didn't bother to look at the report. "I want this drug on the market by winter. We've already started our marketing campaign."

"Sir, this drug was developed as a menopause therapy…"

"I know that. I'm the one who signed for this." Mr. Triplett's voice was getting dangerously quiet.

"Well, it appears that the drug doesn't benefit patients who are already receiving the standard treatment." Ruth placed another report in front of Mr. Triplett. "In addition, it has some serious side effects."

"What kind?"

"Severe kidney disorders."

Mr. Triplett balled his fist. A sign that Ruth was all too familiar with. "Listen, Ruth, I want this product on the market."

"But…"

Mr. Triplett held up his hand. "I don't want any damn excuses. This drug will be available by Christmas."

"What about the FDA?"

Mr. Triplett balled the report up in his hand and threw it across the room. "FDA approval is no problem. You know several members of the approval committee owe me. Hell, I even got Senator Adams, the old Catfish, jumping high hoops for me."

Ruth nodded that she understood.

"I'm holding you personally responsible, Ruth. If this drug fails on the market, you fail!"

"Yes, sir."

Mr. Triplett pointed to the door. "You're excused."

Ruth headed quickly toward the door.

"Oh," Mr. Triplett barked out, "and Ruth."

She turned, still shaken to the core. "Sir?"

"Did you ever find Christopher Miller and the CD's?"

Ruth meekly looked at the floor.

Mr. Triplett remembered the entire scenario as if it were yesterday. "Those damn disks better not see the light of day."

Ruth remained still for a moment and then replied. "They will never surface, sir."

It was time for Ruth to go and find a few underlings to kick. Her reputation as ruthless was about to grow by leaps and bounds.

ATLANTA, GEORGIA

After a long morning meeting with Vance and Quincy, Pamela was glad to make it back to her makeshift office in her Sheraton apartment. It was lunchtime and she was content to just grab a turkey sandwich, potato chips and a Coke and then continue working at her computer. She noticed an icon blinking on the screen. It was her Trojan horse system indicating that an update was needed on computer 2. She opened the icon and tapped into computer 2. It was Bill Barringer's computer. Bill had loaded new data, most likely from the CD he had received the previous evening.

A password was required to open the program. This is when the hacking became fun. She routed the program into a sophisticated code breaker system. A couple of minutes and seven characters, all caps, popped up on the screen. TALLYHO.

She couldn't believe what Bill had in his possession. How in the world did Bill get a document marked confidential from Speck MediSurge?

There was a cover note that told the story. Bill Barringer and Christopher Miller had been fraternity brothers in college.

She spent hours reading the documents. She even forgot about her sandwich. She called Neil and told him to come back to Atlanta. He was on the next flight. This could be their ticket out of everything.

Immediately she passed a computer virus back to Bill's computer. The virus was attached to this program so that when Bill opened it again, the virus would start eating the information as soon as the words TALLYHO were typed into the program. If Bill hadn't made a copy of this information he would lose it all within minutes. Scrambled beyond comprehension. Trashed.

Pamela was oblivious to the world as her fingers tapped across the keyboard of her laptop. The phone rang bringing her back to reality. By the second ring she had snapped out of her trance. She was somewhat surprised when she heard Senator Adams' voice. He wanted Pamela to tell him if there was anything new and important.

"No, nothing new." She lied. The reason she had taken the CD information was not to double-cross Bill, but protect him. If he tried to use it, Pamela knew that Triplett would find him and dish out a handful of pain with no mercy.

The senator told her he was making his move. He planned to call a press conference the next week in Washington to provide a report about the FDA and its improper links with pharmaceutical companies. He would reveal how he was part of an undercover operation conducted by the FBI to uncover the extent of political kickbacks. It was all set. He had all the right people ready to go. And he had all the right sacrificial lambs in place. Nothing had been overlooked. The senator's information would naturally remove any suggestions that he was personally tied to this type of activity.

Pamela knew this day would come. In fact, she had been one of the original designers of the plan. It felt different, though. Or, maybe she was different. She no longer felt good about her history with

Senator Adams. Nor did she feel good about being a double-crossing spy on Vance Connelly. She realized that she respected and admired Connelly. He had a mission in life that was bigger than himself which was something Pamela had never been part of until now.

In addition to the senator's press conference, the senator was going to have Larry Colburn release to the press any information that he had uncovered on Greystone. Colburn would do his part in Atlanta. He was going to set the stage by revealing the information that Pamela had provided earlier about Bill Barringer and his friend who needed a heart transplant. Colburn planned on having the sick, mother of four, that was supposed to receive the next heart, sitting in a wheelchair at the press conference. It was a visual scene created by a crafty lawyer that would leave an unforgettable impression worth millions of dollars.

It would be a two-pronged attack. The senator would coordinate it personally. Everything synchronized, down to the last second. After the press conference the senator would pull out one of his rarest Cuban cigars and slowly smoke it with great pleasure. The Catfish loved to celebrate sweet revenge.

Pamela wasn't ready for everything to start unfolding so quickly. She wanted more time, but knew she was not going to get it. As soon as the senator hung up, she called Quincy and asked him to meet her. She had to act fast.

WASHINGTON, D.C.

The vice president surveyed the cabinet as he gave a summary of the CIA report. International relations were his political mainstay. That's why President Hillgren wanted Lancaster on his ticket. When Lancaster was a senator he had close ties to the CIA and now as vice president he was one of their biggest champions in the White House. But that is exactly why he felt out of step with Hilgren, Lancaster didn't see the domestic agenda as being as important as the international policy.

The president nodded for an assistant to distribute the rough draft of a report on the current state of medicine in America. "Give this document the time it deserves. By next week I want a simple five to six point plan that will act as our medical manifesto for America."

The president called a halt to their meeting. Usually their meeting lasted for hours. Today the president felt worn out.

For weeks the president sensed that something was wrong. He was aware that his fatigue and memory lapses were getting worse. He was fairly certain that others had not yet noticed it, but he surely did. He hated the feeling. He liked to be sharp.

Naturally the president didn't want the press to pick up on anything unusual. Reporters blow everything out of proportion. If the president had a cold they would act as if he had lung cancer. The president had asked Russell to come by. This wouldn't be viewed as unusual by the press. He wanted Russell to examine him. That way the president would be underneath the radar screen of the press hounds.

The president shook his head. He had never shown a modicum of fear to the public. Once he drank water from the disposal pipe of a nuclear power plant, just to demonstrate his confidence in public safety. Despite the "mad cow" epidemic, when he was in England a few weeks earlier he ordered beef wherever they visited. He showcased his faith in the meat for everyone in the world to see.

He wasn't feeling well now, but the president decided to push on as expeditiously as possible until lunch and then take a nap in his private quarters. Then he would call Vance Connelly and invite him to the White House for the weekend.

ATLANTA, GEORGIA

The earliest that Quincy could meet Pamela was around four o'clock, just before rush hour. They decided that it would be easier for Quincy to drop by her apartment. Pamela had a pot of coffee ready for his arrival. They were quick to cut through the trivia and get down to the point at hand. Pamela was set to tell Quincy what the senator was planning.

Pamela sipped her coffee slowly, the tone in her voice had a ring of concern. "I've found out something that I'm going to tell you, but," she put down her coffee and looked him in the eyes, "it's the type of information that you have to handle carefully."

Quincy sat up ready to listen.

Pamela had decided to come clean. She told everything, right down to her role with Senator Adams and Triplett.

Quincy was in a state of disbelief.

"I'm telling you all of this because I want to help and I know how to deal with these men."

Quincy replied sarcastically. "Haven't you helped enough?"

"Quincy," Pamela sighed heavily, "I don't expect you to understand, but I can help you and you do need me."

Pamela explained to Quincy how she had given the senator and Colburn only pieces of information. The senator had built his strategy on a set of distorted half-truths. Together she and Quincy could pull a reversal on the senator. Together they could even take Senator Adams, Triplett and Colburn down altogether. It would be dangerous, but it was possible.

CHAPTER 21

ATLANTA, GEORGIA
OCTOBER 1952

CAMERON PULLED out a cigarette but after a fit of coughing decided to wait a few minutes to light up. Hell, maybe Connelly was right about smoking. He was at home. An empty home. It was another long day and he was about to have a long night. He was there to shower and change.

Cameron kicked off his pants and left them in a heap on the floor. He headed toward the shower. The water bounced off his face and neck as he thought about the Lancaster case and his next move. He stuck his head back under the hot water and let his mind drift for just a moment. Time was of the essence. Sighing, he turned off the shower and dressed. He was ready to head over to see Brooke.

Thirty minutes later Cameron walked up the front steps of Brooke's condo. He noticed the two men in the courtyard.

Brooke answered the door and stood on her toes to look over Cameron's shoulder. One of the men sat in a yard chair reading a newspaper while the other one stood next to a tree, legs spread, hands folded, watching the activity around the condo.

"Friends of yours?" Brooke asked sarcastically.

"No, and they're not the type of people that you would want to take home to meet your mom."

Brooke moved aside. "Who are they?"

"They work for a guy name Evian." Cameron shut the front door. "Somebody that I think you're going to meet and wish you hadn't."

"Why do you think that I'll meet him?" she asked softly.

"He's interested in the Robert Lancaster case." Cameron gave a quick glance around the condo. "Where's your sister?"

"She went to meet Vance at his office. She wants to return to work."

Cameron led Brooke away from the door and sat down with her on the couch. For the next hour Cameron told Brooke about Evian and his interest in the case.

"I didn't know that Robert was involved in that kind of stuff." Brooke stated.

"I don't think that Evian will believe you. He wants his money and he will tap every resource he can. He believes whoever killed Lancaster is responsible for the debt."

Brooke sat on the edge of the couch. She stared hard at the wall in front of them.

Cameron jumped to his feet as the front door slammed against the wall. The sudden noise stopped time for a fraction of a second. It was 11:00 p.m. when the invasion by two armed thugs startled them into silence. Within seconds the thugs were in their faces. Cameron held his hands at shoulder level, palms forward so they would know that he wasn't going for a weapon.

"Boys, take it easy." Cameron said calmly.

One of the thugs approached Cameron, took his gun and then kicked him in the small of his back pushing him toward the door.

"Like I said boys, take it easy." Cameron hated to be pushed.

The other thug motioned for the rest of them to follow Cameron out the door.

"Listen fellas—" Cameron started to say something but was quickly cut off.

"Shut up and keep walking." The thug hammered his gun into Cameron's right kidney.

It was a quiet, uncomfortable ride to James Evian's house. When they arrived, the thugs escorted them down a dark flight of wooden stairs to a room in the basement. The room's walls were cinderblocks painted dark green. The cement floor was pockmarked from heavy use, as if the room had seen a lot of activity over the years. The room was void of furnishings with the exception of two metal chairs with torn leather seats and a sagging couch covered by an ancient stained bedspread. Cameron remained standing. Brooke looked tense as she sat on a chair.

"Like I said, Brooke," Cameron wanted to lighten up the moment, "these people aren't exactly your friendly type."

Brooke arched her right eyebrow as if that was an understatement.

"Brooke," Cameron's voice took on a harsh sound of realism, "don't lie to Evian. Tell him whatever you know."

Another set of thugs stepped into the room. The biggest of the set told them that Evian was ready to see them now.

It was the same room where Cameron had met Evian the first time. Again, Evian was surrounded by his thugs and some business associates. He stood up with a smug grin. "Oh yes, Lieutenant." Evian opened his arms as if to welcome them. "It was so nice of you to come by for another visit. And I see you brought a friend."

Cameron spoke loudly. "You're obstructing justice, not to mention kidnapping!"

Evian smiled at his associates. "Lieutenant, how can the desire to seek the truth be construed as obstruction of justice? And kidnapping? I merely wanted to make sure you could find your way. This is a simple invitation."

Cameron demanded. "Leave us alone, Evian."

A tall heavyset thug gave Cameron a strike in his back, strong enough to make Cameron's knees buckle.

Evian returned to his seat. It was like a throne for a pompous dictator. "I want to know if it's true what I heard." He looked pointedly at Brooke. "Did you kill Lancaster?"

"I don't know anything." Brooke replied immediately.

"Listen Evian." Cameron started to insert.

The thug popped him in the back again.

Cameron felt the sting down to his feet.

Evian waived the thug to back off of Cameron. Like a well-trained Doberman the thug stepped back.

"You're a gambling man." Cameron enticed, massaging his neck.

The statement drew Evian's deepest curiosity.

Cameron continued. "Let's make a bet." He knew that Evian would torture Brooke to find out whatever he wanted to know.

"Now, why on earth should I make a bet when I've got control over all the possibilities here?" Evian looked puzzled.

"Because I'm willing to offer you something you can't resist."

Evian looked at his associates. "And what would that be, Lieutenant?"

"Here's the deal." Cameron slowly got to his feet. "I know that your brother is in prison in Reidsville."

Cameron looked at Evian to see if he had a glimmer of interest. "I can get him out on parole."

Evian face reflected his amusement. "And if I were to lose my bet?"

"Then you and your associates have to give me a chance to find out more about who killed Lancaster."

"Why don't you just speak up, Lieutenant? You are among friends."

"Because you won't believe me without proof."

"What do you mean?"

Cameron restated. "What if I told you that somebody inside your own ranks betrayed you?"

There was a soft clamor of Evian's associates talking over the challenge.

Evian looked at his associates and then laughed. "Someone betrayed me?" Evian knew he had been skillfully maneuvered. He had no choice. "Alright. So what is the game?"

Cameron sighed heavily. "A simple pull of a card. A Jack or higher to win."

Evian laughed. "A man after my own heart." He turned to the group. "He'll stake his life on a draw of a card."

Cameron smiled grimly and waited for the cards to placed in front of him.

Cameron didn't hesitate until he stood over the cards. Slowly, he lifted up his card. It was a Jack of spades.

The entire room hushed, spellbound by the game.

Cameron stood calmly with his hand held high. He showed no fear.

Evian walked quickly to the cards and pulled up his own. Without looking at his card, he held it high to match Cameron.

Perhaps it was fate. Perhaps it was just blind luck of the draw. Evian had drawn a Jack of diamonds.

Cameron won by the draw of a card suit. Spades, hearts, diamonds, clubs. Spades will win every time.

Admitting the loss, Evian dropped his card. "You have ten minutes to prove your case, Lieutenant."

Cameron was still sweating. "Who took Lancaster's bets?"

"Me." Evian replied.

"You directly?" Cameron asked.

"Yes, of course. Anybody that places a bet for $25,000 or more does it directly with me." Evian spoke bitterly. He was perturbed by the loss of the game and it practically choked him to answer questions.

"And his last bet. What was it?" Cameron pressed.

Evian looked at Butterfly. "He liked to bet on the fights. He had $30,000 on the next fight."

"Who were the fighters?" Cameron talked loudly so that Evian's associates could hear.

"Butterfly was fighting." Evian felt his gut turning.

"And do you recall what happened in that fight?" Cameron asked.

Evian looked at his watch. "Your time is up, lieutenant."

"What happened?" Cameron repeated loudly

With his nose flaring wide Evian shouted. "Butterfly lost her first fight."

"There is a reason she lost that fight." Cameron continued to speak loudly. "She had worked a deal with Lancaster. She was on the take."

Everyone in the room stared darkly at Butterfly. She stood quietly, defiantly glaring at everyone who dared look her way.

"Is it true?" Evian demanded.

She met his eyes and said nothing.

Evian shouted at her. "Is it true?"

Butterfly looked down, silently acknowledging her shameful act.

Evian sat down in disbelief. His pride. His love. Butterfly had betrayed him. "Why would you do this?" He asked.

Evian's face hardened, his voice brittle with disappointment. "Why?"

"Because we made a deal." Butterfly looked at Evian with steel in her eyes. "I threw the fight so he could get out of his debt. He in turn would pay me ten grand. I went to the hospital to tell him I wanted my money."

"You did what?" Evian screamed with anger. His face mottled with rage. That fight had cost Evian almost a $100,000.

Butterfly spoke in a low, submissive voice. "He promised the cash but then he double crossed me."

An ominous silence blanketed the room. A silence that made the hair on the back of your neck stand up straight. A manmade, hold your breathe kind of silence that made your lungs forget what to do next.

Cameron took the opportunity to mention that Butterfly was seen at the hospital by a nurse on the night of Robert's death.

No one moved. Only slow collective exhales could be heard.

Butterfly would not look at Evian. She kept her eyes focused on the floor and said nothing.

Evian demanded harshly. "Did you kill him?"

Butterfly looked up to defend herself. "I swear to you I didn't do it." Her face, drawn with bitterness, raised to meet Evian's forthcoming challenging. "Yes, I went there to see him. But not to kill him. I went there to tell him that I wanted my cut of the money, that's all I was going to do, I swear it."

Evian walked toward her. "So he probably told you to take a hike. Why should he give you a dime? What were you going to do, tell me?"

Butterfly shook her head. "No, it was not like that at all."

"Sure. And then when he cut you out of the cash you killed him, didn't you?" Evian was standing within an arm's reach of her.

"No, I tell you that it didn't happen that way."

Evian slapped her across the face. "Don't lie to me bitch!"

Butterfly's impulse was to strike back but she fought off her instinct. "When I went into his room that night he was already dead." Butterfly relived the night. "The window was open and he was already on the ground."

Evian's eyes narrowed as he raised his chin. He inhaled deeply. His own woman had cost him a fortune. His own woman had embarrassed him in front of his men. Now, he didn't believe a word she was saying.

In that instant, Cameron knew that things were about to get out of hand. He knew that they should leave. It was now or never. He turned to Brooke and gave her a nod toward the door. As they started to walk the thugs blocked the way.

Evian quickly turned. At first he was going to have his thugs take care of them but he could feel his associates watching him. He had made a bet. If he backed out on this one, maybe he would back out on one with them. Speaking through his teeth, Evian relinquished. "A bet is a bet. Let them go."

Cameron fought his inclination to arrest Butterfly and walk out of Evian's den with her in handcuffs. He knew though that if he tried that, they would all die. Cameron planned to call for help as soon as they got out of there. He left with visions of Butterfly behind bars, beaten into submission by the toughest broad in the joint. Unfortunately, by the time reinforcements showed up, Evian's house was empty. No cars, no lights, no sign of life.

The next day the police found a young oriental woman floating in the Chattahoochee River. Cameron was at the scene within an hour of the cops finding her body. Now he would never really know what happened with Lancaster. There were a lot of reasons to believe it was Butterfly. But there was one nagging thought that wouldn't let go of him. The bolts. How could she have loosened those bolts? He sure couldn't budge them. So how could a small woman like Butterfly do it?

Sooner or later Cameron was going to get Evian. It took him six months, but true to his pursuit he made sure that Evian was sentenced to prison. Not for the murder of Butterfly, although Cameron had no doubt of his role in her death. The police could never prove that one. Rather, he was indicted for money laundering through Lancaster's bank for an organization known as The Association for Global Opportunity Seekers. Evian's new home became Reidsville Penitentiary, ten cells down from his brother.

Cameron's celebration of justice was short lived. Apparently Cameron was the victim of a hit and run incident. He was leaving Zimbardo's club late one afternoon when a car slammed him into the pavement. After Cameron was rushed to Greystone, Vance tried to save his friend's life but to no avail.

CHAPTER 22

ATLANTA GEORGIA
AUGUST 2001

THE TIME for the big show for the senator and Colburn had come. The meeting was well planned and well attended. The story would lead the national news that evening. The taping was carefully staged in a large conference room in an upscale hotel near Greystone. The television cameras occasionally focused on the upper floors of Greystone giving an impression of a breaking story about the hospital. Senator Adams sported a cheery smile revealing his newly bleached white teeth. He was ready for his appearance.

The senator spoke first. Everyone in the studio thought that his comments were as smooth as a Nat King Cole song on a moonlit night. He gave the best speech of his career and he could feel it just as strongly as he could a winning poker hand. The members of the press took his story hook, line and sinker. He was almost an American hero.

People would be in court for years battling over the senator's lies. For now, though, the senator appeared to have gotten the FBI to mastermind a sting operation to uncover pharmaceutical scams connected with the FDA. Little did the public know that he was the one who instigated the scams in the first place. Yes, the Catfish was back in his old mud hole. Splashing and stirring up everything.

Now it was Larry Colburn's turn.

The master of theatrics set his stage and was ready to go. An exceptionally nice touch was the sick patient, an indigent mother of four. She talked briefly about her family, house and pets. She had been told that she was an ideal candidate for a cardiac transplant and it was her turn for the procedure. She was next in line. She had been promised. Now, she was confused.

She cried out, "I was next in line to receive a new heart. Everyone knows this isn't fair." She shook her hand as she spoke. "Dr. Barringer put another patient in front of me just because I'm poor."

Colburn waived the documents that Pamela had produced. The fake documents that were designed to create confusion. Colburn was quick to assert that lawsuits would be flying for this miscarriage of justice. The members of the press were excited. They knew this was a big story. President Hillgren had chosen Greystone University Hospital as his exemplar case study.

As soon as Colburn finished, a young man stood up near the front and walked toward the center of the conference room. He spoke loudly above the murmur of the press. "Mr. Colburn," The young man yelled confidently.

Colburn singled out the young man in the crowd. He intended to point at him when he recognized who it was. Damn, it was Quincy. How in the world did that joker know anything about today? Colburn's thoughts raced as he tried to direct attention to someone else in the audience.

Quincy spoke loudly. "You may not know it but you are presenting false documents. According to the records, there is actually substantial documentation that shows a different story. A story that shows how you are taking the facts totally out of context. You, or someone, have altered official medical records to build a false case."

A cluster of reporters turned and fired questions at Quincy. As Quincy responded to their questions, Quincy's friend, M Daddy, passed out copies of the documentation to the crowd.

Quincy calmly spoke over the commotion he had stirred. "These copies show that Barringer's initial diagnoses clearly indicated that Jake had severe heart failure due to cardiomyopathy, but his advanced age, excessive alcohol intake, plus being a severe diabetic with kidney complications excluded him from any heart transplant."

Colburn fired back. "When a patient is that sick then why not shoot for a miracle?"

Quincy didn't let Colburn stop him from talking. "The decision was validated by a cross reference to Dr. Connelly who saw Jake in consultation."

"This is what courts are for." Colburn used the microphone to his advantage. "When people have different perceptions and data that conflict with each other, then we let our legal system resolve the dispute."

"This is a perfect example of why medical cost are soaring." Quincy made his way up on to the stage and got close enough to use a different microphone himself. "You're slapping a huge suit on something that doesn't even exist. "

"And who claims that?" Colburn demanded. "The hospital or other doctors? What about the patient's rights?" Shaking his head with anger, Colburn looked at his audience and added. "Do you think they wanted the public to know what they did?"

Quincy held up another document. "I have in my hand, affidavits from over fifteen employees at Greystone. They signed these papers which state in their own words how you contacted them and pressed for information, trying to turn their stories into something that could turn into a lawsuit. Many of them were in the cardiac division and knew the scheduling of heart transplant patients."

Colburn tried to shout down Quincy. "I was doing my job! Of course I asked the hard questions of everyone to get to the bottom of this. This is an enormous social injustice!"

"Then you would have found that the schedule never departed from its original plan." Quincy flagged M Daddy to pass out his document. "There isn't a change by Barringer."

"You bring your witnesses and I'll bring mine!" Colburn was standing his ground.

Quincy smiled at Colburn and faced the reporters. "I hope that the press studies my documents closely because they include four employees who reveal that you attempted to pay them substantial funds to tell you what you wanted to hear."

Colburn stared hard at Quincy.

"So if we must waste time and money, and slander good names in court, I guess we'll see you there." Quincy started back down the platform, carrying the attention of the press as he exited.

Colburn's press conference was a piece of magician's flash paper, a momentary flame and then nothing but ashes. Colburn knew that he had been set up. He also knew it was time to say no more. He watched as the reporters slowly streamed out the exit. His mind traced rapidly through all the events. Pamela. Yes, it had to be Pamela.

That evening, the national news only showed Senator Adams. The Colburn case was a dead story. Dead cold. And Colburn not only lost his credibility, but Greystone was gearing up to sue him for misrepresentation of facts and false accusations. The tables had turned and they had turned on Colburn. He was sure that Senator Adams would distance himself from this fiasco. Adams wouldn't dare ask Colburn to return the money. He would deny knowing anything about this episode. There was no proof of any connection between the two men.

Colburn didn't have to plan his next flight out of Atlanta. He would take the next available flight to Washington D.C. Atlanta had left a bad taste in his mouth and he wanted to forget the whole damn thing. It was going to take a lot of martinis to forget this day.

ATLANTA, GEORGIA

Quincy relayed the entire episode to Pamela. She let out a delicious laugh as she pictured Colburn's face. She also knew that this was her defining moment. The moment from which there was no turning back. The senator and Colburn didn't like betrayal and they would deal with her accordingly. She was now on the run. For the rest of her life she would be looking over her shoulder. Her only alternative was to get out of the country and do it quickly. Neil Henry would go with her.

Before flying to Atlanta to join Pamela, Neil met with Vice President Lancaster. Although the vice president didn't know it, this meeting would be the last time he would see Neil's face. Not that Lancaster cared. When Neil left the vice president's office he handed Lancaster a package of documents that would make very interesting nighttime reading material.

The documents revealed the truth about Lancaster's staged car accident so many years ago. They detailed how Senator Adams put Neil Henry in charge of faking the events that unfolded. Neil Henry and Senator Adams had picked the night, place, time and people to pull off what could have been a scene in an action movie. Neil Henry included the names of all those involved, what their roles were, how much they were paid and where they were presently living.

No longer would the Vice President owe any favors. No longer would he have to worry about an old skeleton popping out of his closet and up on the press radar, ruining his career. He was free.

The next morning Neil and Pamela locked arms together and walked into the Atlanta International Airport. They bought tickets to hopscotch their way through three potential routes. They would make their final decision of where to land at the last possible moment. Neil favored the route that took them from Atlanta to New York, bouncing through Los Angles and Hawaii before jetting back to Canada. Alberta, Canada was God's country to Neil. Pamela didn't care. She was just happy to leave.

They sat in the Delta Crown Room drank an early morning Bloody Mary. Neil and Pamela had collected a lot of Speck MediSurge stock over the years. They waited for the stock market to open so they could make some heavy transactions.

"You know if they ever catch us," Neil said seriously, "we're dead."

Pamela nodded remembering the story that Triplett told the senator about the guy in his "Association" that got his throat slit and his tongue pulled out through it like a tie. "Yeah, to think, we were scared of the senator." Pamela put her hand into Neil's hand and squeezed tightly. "Hell, the senator is a cream puff compared to Triplett."

"Our only hope is get to Triplett first." Neil looked at his watch. It was 9:15 a.m. Time to call their broker and then draw straws for their final destination.

After finalizing all transactions, they took time to review their plan to stop Triplett. Within forty-eight hours after their departure, a close friend of Pamela's would give the New York Times full disclosure of the Jorestat research that Christopher Miller had died to reveal. It would be clear that Speck MediSurge had committed acts that warranted investigation for criminal conduct. The FBI would confiscate the Speck MediSurge research and financial files.

Neil was glad they had gotten their money out of Speck MediSurge. "After the Times runs their story, how much do you think Speck MediSurge stock will drop?"

"I'd guess seventy percent the first week." Pamela surmised.

"Do you know how heavily the "Association" was invested in Speck MediSurge?"

"I'm sure they had several hundred million dollars invested."

Neil shook the cubes in his glass. "I wonder how Triplett is going to explain that?"

Pamela pictured Triplett's anger when he realized how he had been double-crossed. "If he's smart he won't hang around and try to explain anything. He best be on the run."

WASHINGTON, DC
AUGUST 2001

By Friday afternoon the president had been working almost nonstop. He didn't recognize weekends as a time to rest. He saw it as a time to catch up on his workload while the rest of the country paused for 48 hours. He almost always worked seven days a week, even when he was fatigued, bone-tired and frustrated.

The president was sitting behind his desk in the Oval Office talking with the Vice President when Vance entered. The president had called Vance to come for the weekend to give an update on the progress of the subcommittee.

The president smiled warmly and asked Vance to make himself comfortable.

The vice president handed them a report filled with statistics. The latest polls. "We're scoring big right now, Mr. President. It's not often that a president carries a popularity vote this high on domestic issues."

The President was proud of his ratings. He looked at Vance. "I think it's time to use some of my political capital on our health care reform."

The vice president chimed into the conversation. "I've been reading the reports you've provided. Your ideas are intriguing."

This was the first time the vice president seemed to engage Vance in conversation. Perhaps Vance was hypersensitive about the past. Sure, 1952 was a long time ago. But, then again, Vance was the primary reason that the Lancaster Bank of America had a lot of bad publicity. When the press released the story of the money laundering activity involving the vice president's uncle, Robert Lancaster, their family bank was almost destroyed. Fortunately for the family, the bank survived and over time grew substantially.

The vice president asked Vance to give an overview of his plan.

"My subcommittee has a clear goal." Vance stated with conviction. "We want to eliminate the effort made to turn medicine into a business. All individuals should carry a health card. The physician then sends the bill to a single payer."

The Vice President interrupted Vance. "And where will the money come from?"

"The money supporting the single payer will be a mixture of private and public funds," Vance replied knowing that this would be at the heart of future issues. "Of course, you need the appropriate watchdogs to ensure the proper use of the system. But the important points are that we take the doctor out of doing the paperwork and that we don't use sick people for profit."

The President didn't respond to the underlying fiscal concerns the vice president was voicing; instead he picked up on the surface meaning of the message to move their discussions forward. "I couldn't agree with you more." The President started to pick up a cup of coffee. Unfortunately, the coffee never made it to his mouth. With a short jerky action, the president knocked it over. A naïve observer wouldn't even think twice about what happened. A little coffee spilled, that's all. But, Vance wasn't a naïve observer. He noticed the abrupt jerk of the arm before the hand neared the coffee.

Vance's left eye squinted tightly as he continued to observe the president.

That was the only sip of coffee the president took during their meeting. They spent the rest of their time talking over Vance's ideas for the President's health care reform plan.

LAWRENCEVILLE, GEORGIA

A cloud of dust followed the well-equipped ambulance as it hurried down the gravel driveway. The red lights flashed brightly against the darkness of the early morning. It was a quiet time of day. Everything was still. When the paramedics entered the house Connie escorted them into Jake's room. The dull illumination of a soft lamplight lit the room.

Bill was hovered over Jake checking his pulse. Jake's pulse was weak and his breathing shallow. Bill had found Jake motionless. It was Bill's habit to frequently check on Jake. He would slip by Jake's bedroom door and listen for the familiar sound of snoring. The same old noisy sound always filled the room. This time there was an eerie wheezing sound. It alerted Bill enough for him to enter the bedroom and turn on the light next to Jake's bed. Bill knew immediately that Jake was dying.

Jake's heart beat sporadically. His eyes were shut and in the dim light his face carried a peaceful expression.

Bill watched as the paramedics lifted Jake gently onto the gurney and he followed them to the ambulance. Still in his pajamas, bathrobe and slippers, Bill crawled in and sat hovering over his old friend. Bill would try everything he knew. He tried all the way to the emergency room. Jake never stirred.

Bill whispered to Jake, knowing that he wouldn't respond. It was too painful for Bill to cry. His gut twisted. His memories raced. There was nothing he could do. All of his training was useless. Bill's frustration only grew as they approached the hospital. Two minutes away from the emergency room, Jake exhaled his last breath. Jake was dead on arrival. Bill called Connie with the news. His voice was dull with exhaustion. His spirit was drained.

Jake was gone.

WASHINGTON, D.C.

That evening at dinner Vance got his second clue concerning the President's health.

The President was in the middle of polishing off an impressive mound of pecan brownie, homemade ice cream and fudge sauce. He was listening to a joke that one of the senators at the dinner was telling when he spooned some ice cream. The ice cream never made it to his mouth. His right arm did a slight jerk and the ice cream landed on the table.

The senator telling the joke was quick to say, "Mr. President, I haven't even told the punch line yet."

Everyone gave a polite laugh. As the senator finished telling his joke a waiter brought a wet cloth to clean up the ice cream.

The President gave a quick glance at the First Lady to gauge her response.

In that one moment, Vance knew that the President had called him to the White House for more than just an update on his subcommittee.

After dinner the First Lady asked Vance and Russell to join her on the Truman balcony while the President continued talking with the guests.

Russell broke the ice. "Vance, I think you know why we asked you up for the weekend."

Vance nodded. "I think I've figured it out."

"For the most part I don't think my Dad's symptoms have been noticed by others." Russell said softly.

"It won't be long." Vance replied.

The First Lady recalled his initial symptoms. "About two months ago he started having occasional jerks in his arms."

"But it's getting more frequent and severe?" Vance asked.

"Yes." The First Lady's face showed her concern.

"Does he have trouble with his memory?" Vance remembered the time that the President struggled to recall Vance's name.

"I have to remind him of names that he should know." The First Lady clasped her hands tightly. "He forgot the name of our chief chef the other day."

"I take it the chef isn't a new employee?"

"No, he has served us the entire time we've been here." The First lady replied.

"We want you to examine my Dad," Russell expressed an air of urgency. "We need to know what is happening and if we can help."

"And if we can't?" Vance asked sternly.

"My husband loves America, Vance." The First Lady announced. "He would do nothing to hurt this Country."

"My father would like us to meet him at 7:00 a.m. tomorrow in the Oval Office." Russell added carefully. "You should conduct yourself as if it is just a routine report to the President."

Vance smiled. It was a comforting assured smile that always relieved the tension of those who seemed concerned.

The fresh air felt good as Vance started to think about his new patient. "I would like for the President to go over some material tonight." Vance prescribed. "I will review the material with him tomorrow."

Russell recognized that Vance had devised a memory test.

Looking at his watch, Russell said. "I'll go over it line by line with him."

Before calling it a night, Vance told Russell, "There is one other thing I need to tell you."

Russell could sense the urgency in Vance's voice.

Vance gave a short version of the 1952 story. He told Russell about Robert Lancaster and the mob. Then he asked if Russell could arrange for him to view the Goodroe tape to zoom on to Triplett's ring.

Russell promised that it would happen as soon as possible. At last Russell was able to pull some strings for his old mentor.

The next morning Vance entered the Oval Office, creating a serious, still air. Russell stood next to his father. Both were silent.

It was not a long or extensive checkup, but it was tense. Vance didn't find anything that he hadn't already anticipated. The president felt extremely tired and had occasional, but definite moments of memory loss, especially for recent events. In addition, the President believed his memory was deteriorating rapidly. He couldn't remember much of the document that Russell had discussed with him the night before.

"I need to ask you something, Mr. President." Vance asked as he continued his exam.

"What's that?" The President replied.

"Why did you want me to conduct this check-up?" Vance asked.

"Because," the President replied, "Russell gave me the article you wrote about presidential disabilities."

Vance looked at the president with a question mark written on his face.

"I never know what is going to stick in my memory. For some reason the paper you wrote is firmly imprinted in my mind, but the material I read last night is not."

Vance wasn't sure himself why some events or memories could be recalled and others fell by the wayside. "I was responding to a study that was reported in the same journal. The study revealed that today's world leaders remained in office after having coronary events including heart attacks."

"As I recall, the authors studied newspaper accounts about the coronary events that occurred in world leaders." The president remembered the article quite well.

Vance nodded. "Their study also implied that world leaders don't hide illnesses from the press as they did years ago."

"Nowadays, we tell 'em everything. Hell, we even have a former senator promoting Viagra on television."

"We tell the public most things." Vance replied. "Illnesses like gall bladder disease, thyroid trouble, cancer, and even stroke, but…"

"But," the president interrupted, "as you pointed out in your article, certain neurological and psychiatric diseases don't tend to get reported."

Russell had been sitting quietly, taking in the conversation. "That's because some of those conditions aren't very obvious and it can be difficult to make a diagnosis."

The president hung his head. "I know that I have serious problem."

There was a long pause. Nobody spoke.

Although there was more diagnostic work to be done, the president would soon have to make a decision about how he was going to handle this situation if the worst were confirmed. He could try to hide it. Maybe he could even get away with it for a short time. But with his memory getting rapidly worse he couldn't keep the secret much longer.

Vance wrapped up his examination. "I want to call in a neurologist." Vance crossed his arms in front of his chest. "The man I believe is the foremost expert in the world is located in Boston."

The President looked at Vance. "Any clue as to what's happening with me?"

"You have some type of neurodegenerative disease, but I think we can eliminate one thing." Vance put his hand on the president's shoulder. "We can discount Alzheimer's. I have never heard of a patient with Alzheimer's who also has myoclonic jerks and whose memory loss has progressed so rapidly."

The President stared blankly for a moment. "Russell, I'll tell your mother what's happening. In the meantime, I don't want to be in limbo over this. Let's get the neurologist in as fast as we can."

"I'll send the helicopter for him." Russell said as he stood.

After leaving the Oval office, Vance called the neurologist in Boston. His wife answered the phone. She told Vance that her husband had gone camping with their son and that he wouldn't be back until Sunday. She knew vaguely where their campsite was located. The neurologist didn't take his cell phone. He was trying to get away from everything.

Secret Service agents were dispatched in a helicopter within the hour. Their mission was to find the neurologist and bring him back to the White House. ASAP.

The helicopter returned to the White House later that day. The neurologist stepped out of the chopper still dressed in his plaid shirt and jeans.

CHAPTER 23

ATLANTA, GEORGIA
AUGUST 2001

FIRST CLASS was the only way to travel as far as Pamela and Neil were concerned. They sat back and relaxed while discussing their plans. Their first stop would be New York City. They'd spend a few days there and then fly to Los Angeles. Their final destination was planned but they weren't on any timetable. They could even change their minds and drop their initial plans and go by impulse. Who knows where or when they would stop for sure?

Pamela sat back and reflected on their escape from the Catfish and Triplett. "Did I tell you that I went by and saw my brother?"

"The Reverend?" Neil asked.

"Yes. Hard to believe my brother Josh is a minister."

Neil laughed. "Did it give him a heart attack seeing you just pop in on him?"

"No." Pamela replied. "As a matter of fact, he said that he saw me that day I visited his church. He said that he had been looking for me every Sunday since."

Neil flagged the flight attendant and asked for two more Bloody

Mary's.

Pamela continued. "I figured that since you and I were leaving I wouldn't need my material assets."

Neil flashed a look of disbelief. "Don't tell me you signed over your property!"

Pamela nodded. "I gave the assets to the church."

"You mean to tell me that you signed over your Washington condo?"

"Yep."

"And the property you worked so hard to finagle from Senator Adams?"

"Yep."

"Pamela, that was water-front property on the Gulf! It was worth nearly half a million!"

"That's pocket change to us now." Pamela replied.

The flight attendant handed them their drinks. Neil took a big gulp. "That's a whole lot of pocket change, dear!"

Pamela was relieved that she had that moment with her brother and she was relieved to know that he had never judged her. He only prayed for her. "I also gave him our insurance."

"What insurance?"

"I gave Josh all the files stored on Senator Adams." Pamela gloated over the idea. "I also told him to tell Bill Barringer that he would never have to fear the Catfish. We are all well protected. Then, I e-mailed the senator and told him that if anything happens to any of us, the files would be given to the FBI."

When their flight landed, the first thing Pamela wanted to do was buy a bagel topped with cream cheese. For some reason bagels have a different taste when they're made in the Big Apple. This was the perfect start for their new life. For Pamela and Neil, today was Day One of freedom.

WASHINGTON, DC.

The White House physician, Vance and the neurologist, a prominent expert on neurodegenerative diseases, spent Saturday afternoon examining the President. Their conclusion wasn't good. Although they weren't one hundred percent sure, they believed that the President was afflicted with a Creutzfeldt-Jakob type disease, simply referred to as CJ disease.

The personal residence at the White House had a gloomy air. For hours the president and First Lady kept their privacy. For a while, Russell was kept at bay but he eventually was allowed to join them. Soon the president's closest advisors and friends were streaming into the White House. One by one they each left with a heavy heart. The White House staff and reporters could sense that something serious was happening, especially since the president didn't work that evening.

On Sunday, the vice president and the president's cabinet was called to the White House for a closed door meeting. That afternoon, a press conference was called.

Anyone in politics knows several basic rules. First, always announce bad news on Friday afternoon. This way the public has time to adjust to their initial emotions. Besides, the stock market can't react until Monday and that gives time for the "spin doctors' to paint their perception. Second, never call a press conference on Sunday afternoon when the NFL and AFL are scheduled to play. Interrupting Sunday afternoon football would blow millions for the networks. A Sunday afternoon press conference had better be significant.

Reporters lined the walls of the pressroom at the White House. A soft murmur of voices vibrated through the room. The reporters noted the impressive members of the audience. The cabinet members, Supreme Court judges and the vice president were present. Just as the whispering and curiosity of the reporters reached a peak, the hour arrived. The president, First Lady and Russell began their walk down the red carpet that led to the lectern. Soon the president stood behind the lectern, waiting for the First Lady to be seated.

The president looked from right to left and gave his now familiar smile. "I appreciate your attendance on this short notice, but I have something to tell you and the American people that I feel cannot wait." The President pulled out a small note from his pocket to read. "A free and responsible press is an essential element of a democracy and I have enjoyed our relationship. What I have to share with you now is as personal as it can be, but it influences every person in this country."

President Hillgren always carried an aura as thick and strong as any leader in history. After meeting the President, E. B. Goodroe, the famous news commentator, said, "You can feel an energy buzzing around that man as strong as a spooked hornet's nest." Tonight, President Hillgren projected a force that even the people in the back of the room could sense. The television sets of America radiated the power and the strength of the president.

"One of the greatest features of a responsible person is to accept the fact that he or she must act responsible at all times. There must be no exception." Turning to Vance the president said, "It is comparable to the responsibility a physician has for his or her patients. Theirs is a responsibility that has nothing to do with any other emotion or reward, it is simply the act of a truly responsible person."

The president paused and let the reporters absorb his comments.

"I am clearly in that position now. I have talked with my wife, doctors, friends and advisors. And I have made my decision."

The president put away his notes and spoke from his heart. "The fact is, I have been having episodes of memory loss and I believe they are becoming more frequent. I also realize that my arms occasionally jerk so I knock over glasses and cups. The doctors," the president tried to lighten the moment a little, "will later tell you some of the fancy names that they call my trouble."

The president took a quick pause to drink a sip of water. Again he looked across the room and gave his comfort smile. He knew that everyone was hanging onto every word.

"The doctors pointed out that it was too early to diagnose a specific condition. However, they believe I have a progressive type of neurodegenerative disease."

Immediately there was buzz of noise in the room. The president held his hand for silence. The room quieted as quickly as it had escalated into momentary chaos.

The reporters were stunned. Ordinarily hands would be shooting up to ask questions. But instead, there was silence.

"Because I love this country I know that I can't take chances on making a bad decision that could cause injury. Therefore," the president stood tall, "I resigned the presidency a few hours ago. The appropriate letters have been signed and sent to those who must be notified."

Never before had the press appeared so shocked. They sat completely dumbfounded.

"Approximately one hour ago in a small and private ceremony, Vice President Lancaster took the oath of office for president of the United States of America. The ceremony took place in the Oval Office. The event was captured on tape that will be distributed to you as soon as possible. It is my hope and prayer that our new president will carry on the important legislation that we have initiated. President Lancaster has been a wonderful supporter and friend." The former president waived for President Lancaster to approach the lectern. They shook hands and hugged for a brief period. Former President Hillgren leaned into the microphone. "Carry on, Mr. President. Carry on."

After a brief statement the new president asked Vance Connelly, the White House physician and the neurologist to discuss the condition that they believed might be present and to answer questions posed by the members of the press.

The former president, his wife and son then walked the red carpet for the last time.

The members of the press, although still in shock, stood slowly and applauded for several minutes. They had witnessed the changing of the guard. A new president. A peaceful transition. Hillgren was a good man whose place in history would shine forever.

———◆———

The evening news carried a full report about CJ disease. Vance and the neurologist had done their best to address questions from the press. The network only broke away once to show the White House helicopter leaving with the former president and his family. They would go to Andrews Air Base and board a special jet. Destination, Georgia.

By Monday the papers were loaded with news. The report that President Lancaster would keep the present cabinet and advisors bode well with the press. President Lancaster had quickly taken hold of the political reins of power. He announced that he would continue with the Hillgren agenda for the future of America. He particularly wanted to continue to reform the health care system. He announced that Vance Connelly would remain his senior health care advisor. By late afternoon on Monday the entire country was struggling to adjust their feelings. The pain was evident across the nation. Soon one of the tabloids put it's inevitable spin of ruthless imagination to it's headline:

PRESIDENT HILLGREN RESIGNS BECAUSE OF MAD COW DISEASE

The reporter and editor of this popular tabloid ignored the discussion given at the press conference by the neurologist who had pointed out carefully that the ground beef President Hillgren consumed during his London trip was not responsible for his illness. The doctor repeated several times that the time between eating the beef in London to the signs of the disease was far too short for there to be a relationship. He stressed that many months, even years, pass before symptoms of a disease like CJ develop after "exposure" to the damaged nerve protein found in beef. But the tabloids could smell the money from this story. They were in the headline hunt and were determined to have a field day.

On the flight back to Atlanta Vance read three newspapers, each with it's own set of predictions about what this would mean for the country. For now, everything was up in the air. Press the pause button and hope that the reverse button is not engaged. Health care could once again take a back seat to other political agendas. But, he thought as he half smiled to himself, that is the nature of our political system.

Still in the midst of this political turmoil Vance read an article about a division of one of the country's largest makers of medical devices and how it had to plead guilty to 14 felonies. The CEO of the company admitted that he had lied to the FDA and hid thousands of serious health problems including nearly a dozen deaths, caused by one its products. The company stock was taking a nose dive, key executives were going to be tried and a fine of over 100 million dollars in criminal and civil penalties were going to be imposed for failing to report problems to the government.

Vance folded the paper and placed it aside in anger. He took off his glasses and rubbed his tired eyes. He thought about the future and what it would take to create change because without it happening soon, this type of problem was only going to get worse. Corruption and greed were becoming the norm.

Vance's last thoughts before he fell asleep was that everybody has a role in this mess in some way. Each person in this country would have to make a decision on where they stand. His role was to stay in the battle and keep stirring the pot until the health care system was beyond politics or business or medical corruption, but focused on the care of sick people.

EPILOGUE

ATLANTA, GEORGIA
DECEMBER 2001

ANOTHER LONG day had passed for Vance and he was nearly exhausted. Although it had been several months since Hilgren had stepped down the press was still calling. Most wanted to know if President Lancaster was continuing the charge on health care or was his agenda for America different. The verdict was still out. For now President Lancaster was reviewing everything. Others wanted to know more about Hilgren's condition and how we can ensure presidential competency in the future.

By the time Vance settled back in his favorite chair and flipped on the news, the doorbell rang. It felt like he was crawling to the door. Two men, both with serious faces, were standing in a small huddle. After they showed Vance their FBI badges, he led them into the living room where they went through more formal introductions.

They wanted to know why Vance had asked Russell to get the FBI involved. Vance explained that one day he was sitting in his thinking chair at 4:00 am when his mind drifted back to 1952. He saw Cameron in his mind's eye. His old friend was telling him about the evidence-the bolts-the dust on the window sill-a stand alone speck of glass. Cameron's image was telling Vance about Tripletts ring and when he first saw it the day that Big Ron was officially initiated into the mob. That's when Vance suddenly put it together. Perhaps the speck wasn't glass. Perhaps it was part of a ring. It was a long shot, but worth checking out. Sometimes his best findings about a disease started with a simple hunch.

Apparently Triplett's ring did tell a story of its own. From the Goodroe tape the FBI was able to determine that there was a small chip missing in the gem part of Triplett's ring then they pulled the evidence from 1952 and ran through a series of test. They found a small chip of gem snagged in the evidence. Computer simulation showed that it was a perfect match with Tripletts ring.

The only thing that the FBI could not figure out was Triplett's motive.

Vance thought about the conversations he had with Cameron. He remembered how Cameron described the celebration he attended at Evian's. A celebration that marked Triplett's advancement in the Association. Triplett was the up and coming leader of Evian's part of the Association. He was the chosen one to take the place of Evian. What if he didn't want to wait to work his way up the ladder? What if, in his youth, he was in a hurry to take over that region? All of these thoughts would never be known but they made a good argument.

Vance explained his theory to the FBI. They scribbled a few notes and told him that he would be dragged into a lengthy court situation. Apparently they were going to go after Triplett.

SPRING 2002

By the beginning of the New Year everything changed for America. The priorities for President Lancaster's administration were no longer on domestic affairs. The president called Vance personally to tell him that all of the health care reform efforts would be put on hold.

America had to focus on a long war against terrorism and on homeland security.

After finding out from Neil Henry that Senator Adams was the mastermind of the car accident scam so many years ago, President Lancaster made sure that the Catfish was ostracized by his strongest political supporters. That too would be a long campaign for President Lancaster because the Catfish always had a way to spin a situation. This time was no different. The Catfish was down, but never counted out.

Tripplett was arrested and was set for his court trials. Mysteriously, while in jail they found Triplett with his throat cut. He had his own Columbian necktie.

Speck MediSurge announced a new CEO. The employees of the company were now answering to a woman they had nicknamed, Ruthless.

Bill and Connie were talking about packing up everything and moving away from Atlanta. They thought it was best to bring little John up in a rural town. Perhaps a small town in Montana. Bill and Connie had dreamed about opening a small medical clinic. Connie would even return to doctoring. And, of course, they would take their horses with them.

Neil and Pamela were still on the run. They would never be heard from again.

Quincy stayed his course. He continued his residency in internal medicine at Greystone. After that he planned to do a fellowship that would give him experience in research. Someday, Quincy would enter academic medicine and be a chairman of the department of medicine himself. For now, as long as Vance was able and willing, Quincy would continue to meet with his friend and mentor. Quincy knows he still has a lot to learn.

Greystone University School of Medicine and Greystone University Hospital continue to rank with the best and new buildings spring up with surprising speed. Once in a rare while, a young doctor will be seen tagging the marble entrance sign. Inevitably, those young doctors end up in Vance Connelly's office.

Much to Jennifer's dismay, Vance continues to go to work everyday. He writes long hours and teaches eight sessions each week. In character and spirit, Vance jokingly tells everyone that he will continue as long as his creative juices flow and as long as his memory is better than the students and house staff. He knows, of course, that some day he will reach for a memory or a new idea and they will not be there, but for now they are still there—quick, accurate and complete!

Each part of the health care system continues to be tarnished as the corruption grows.